My Life As a
Torpedo Test Target

the incredible worlds of
Wally McDoogle

My Life As a Torpedo Test Target

BILL MYERS

Illustrations by Jeff Mangiat

Tommy nelson™
for tweens and teens

A Division of Thomas Nelson Publishers
Since 1798

www.thomasnelson.com

Published in Nashville, Tennessee, by Tommy Nelson®, a Division of
Thomas Nelson, Inc. Visit us on the Web at www.tommynelson.com.

Tommy Nelson® books may be purchased in bulk for educational, busi-
ness, fund-raising, or sales promotional use. For information, please
email SpecialMarkets@ThomasNelson.com.

Scripture quotations in this book are from the *International Children's
Bible*®, *New Century Version*®, © 1986, 1988, 1999 by Tommy Nelson®, a
Division of Thomas Nelson, Inc. All rights reserved.

Library of Congress Cataloging-in-Publication Data

Myers, Bill, 1953–
   My life as a torpedo test target / Bill Myers ; illustrations by Jeff
Mangiat.
     p. cm.— (The incredible worlds of Wally McDoogle ; 6)
   Summary: Twelve-year-old Wally learns an important lesson
about greed after a mishap-filled adventure involving sea crea-
tures, pirates, a sunken submarine, and a misguided torpedo.
   ISBN 0-8499-3538-5 (trade paper)
   ISBN 1-4003-0638-8 (hardcover)
   [1. Underwater exploration—Fiction. 2. Christian life—Fiction.
3. Humorous stories.] I. Title. II. Series: Myers, Bill, 1953–   .
PZ7.M98234Myn 1994
[Fic]—dc20   93–47259
                                           CIP
                                           AC

Printed in the United States of America
05 06 07 08 09 WRZ 9 8 7 6 5 4 3 2 1

To Laura Minchew and Beverly Phillips—
For letting me play.

"Be careful and guard against
all kinds of greed."
—Luke 12:15

Contents

Chapter 1

Just for Starters

I sat on the deck of the ship as it pitched to-and-fro and fro-and-to. Back-and-forth and forth-and-back. It's not that I was getting seasick or anything. It's just that the breakfast I'd eaten earlier was doing a pretty good imitation of leapfrog—a leapfrog that was definitely wanting to leap out of my stomach.

I had to do something to take my mind off all the internal action. I reached down and snapped on Ol' Betsy, my laptop computer. It was time to write another one of my famous superhero stories. Now, you're probably wondering how I got here and all that stuff. I promise to tell you in a couple of minutes. But if I don't hurry up and think about a story, this morning's breakfast will definitely be making an encore appearance. . . .

It was a dark and stormy night. (Is there any other type in these kinds of stories?) The rain rained, the hail hailed, and the lightning er...uh... *lightninged*.

Our superhero, the world-famous Gnat Man, sits in his Gnat Cave reading his latest issue of *Popular Pesticides*. (Hey, when you're the world's only superhero insect, you gotta keep up on the latest bug sprays.) Suddenly, the Gnat Phone rings.

Buzzz-buzzz, buzzz-buzzz.

He picks it up and answers. "Hello, Superheroes Unlimited. If you've got the dimes, we'll solve the crimes."

"Gnat Man!" a voice cries. "It's me, your favorite sidetick!"

"Flea Boy?" our hero asks. "What's wrong? Listen, if it's about the five bucks I owe you, I promise——"

"No, Gnat Man, it's worse."

"You're not still sore about that flea collar I sent you for Christmas! It was supposed to be a joke. How'd I know your mother would wear it? Besides, I sent flowers to the funeral, so you can't be too——"

"No, Gnat Man, it's even worse than that."

"You don't mean?"

"Yes!" Suddenly, there is a blast of scary music—the type you always hear in these superhero stories. "Your archrival, the proverbial Proverb Guy, has escaped from the Prison for the Criminally Inane (translation: the Stupidiously Silly Funny Farm)!"

"And he's coming after me?"

"Yes. The guy's bought every can of Raid from here to the Mexican border."

"Well, thanks for the warning, Flea Boy—"

"But there's more!"

"He's not buying those nasty fly strips, too?"

"No...while in prison, Proverb Guy developed a special magnetic device called an Excuse-a-tron. It collects all of the world's excuses."

"You don't mean—"

"That's right. Soon he'll be the sole owner of every excuse ever made. No one will be able to make another excuse for anything again."

Our hero gasps a heroic gasp. "You mean kids will never be able to make the excuse that they're late because the alarm didn't go off?"

"That's right."

"Or that they didn't floss their teeth because they couldn't find that little floss container their dentist gave them at the last checkup?"

"Yup."

"Or that they don't have their homework because their dog ate it?"

"You've got it. There will be no excuses for anything!"

"This is terrible!" our hero cries.

"That's why we need your help, Gnat Man."

"I'd love to help, Flea Boy, but... but..."

"But what?"

"Well I was going to make the excuse that the Gnat Mobile is in for repairs, but I can't seem to get the words out."

"That's because he's stealing everyone's excuses! It's so bad that politicians around the country are actually having to keep their promises!"

Suddenly, there is a loud crackle on the other end of the phone and a strange voice speaks: "Greetings, Gnat Man."

Our super superhero shudders a shuddering shudder. He recognizes the voice instantly. It can be none other than (more bad-guy music)...*Proverb Guy!*

The voice is cool and calm:

"Confucius say,
'Man who live in glass house,
should dress in basement.'"

"Proverb Guy!" our hero shouts. "Is that you?"

The voice does not answer the question, but recites another proverb:

"Man who carry ladder to class, probably goes to *high* school."

"All right, all right!" Gnat Man shouts. "Just tell me what you want."

"I want *you!*" the voice sneers. "I want you on the corner of Olympic Avenue and Main Street at high noon...or no one will ever be able to make another excuse again."

"But...but..." Gnat Man wants to say something like, he has to get a haircut, or he has to wash his shoelaces, or that he's allergic to dying (he breaks out in a bad case of death every time it happens). But he cannot squeeze out a single excuse. "All right!" he finally cries. "I'll be there!"

Proverb Guy begins to chuckle... then to laugh...then he throws himself down on the floor in hysteria. "You're mine, you little insectoid...all mine!"

Our hero slams down the phone and races to the closet to throw on his Gnat Cape. Soon he will know what evil awaits. Soon he will come face to face with the dastardly Excuse-a-tron.

Gnat Man hops in his Gnat Mobile, shifts it into "Superfly," and buzzes out of the Gnat Cave, when suddenly—"

"Hey, McDoogle! Are you coming into the water or what?"

I looked up from Ol' Betsy. I hate being interrupted in the middle of writing one of my stories. But floating in the water below me were my two best friends, Wall Street and Opera. They wore their scuba gear and were splashing around beside the boat.

"Come on!" they shouted. "Hurry up and get in!"

I gave a heavy sigh. The only thing I hated worse than stopping in the middle of my stories was drowning in the middle of the Pacific Ocean. But, by the looks of things, that was next on my list.

Don't get me wrong. I'm a pretty decent swimmer. In fact, during the last couple of days, I'd even gotten the hang of using the face mask and scuba tank. It's just when you put the possibility of anything going wrong and me, Wally McDoogle, in the same room (or ocean), the chances of something catastrophic happening are pretty high. It's like a law or something. If you're looking for a disaster, just make sure I'm around.

Okay, like I promised, I'll fill you in on how we got here. It's kind of complicated, but the big picture goes like this:

Opera's uncle, Captain Raymond Alexander, and his crew are trying to find an old sunken World War II submarine. But it isn't the submarine they are interested in. It's the gold someone is supposed to have stolen and hidden inside the sub. Some guy ripped off a drug ring down in Mexico. He traded the money for gold, melted it into bars, and sailed his ship out here. Then he hid the bars in an old submarine that was rumored to have sunk in the area years ago—a submarine supposedly guarded by some prehistoric monster.

Got all that? Good, 'cause there's more . . .

Unfortunately, the guy never lived to tell where the submarine was. A few weeks ago he had sailed his boat, *The Peacock*, into this area all by himself to hide the gold, but he never came back. They never found him or *The Peacock*. All they had was his last radio transmission. It was majorly weird. He only broadcasted three words. *"Beware the Stinger."* That was all, just *"Beware the Stinger."* And then he signed off.

No one knows what happened to him. He could have died from foul play, hungry sharks, or even that strange monster reported to be in the area. Any way you look at it, these next few days, off the coast of Mexico, definitely spelled *adventure*. Unfortunately, every time I try to spell *adventure* it comes out

D-i-s-a-s-t-e-r

The three of us were pretty jazzed about Captain Ray's letting us work as crew members. "There will be no pay," he had explained. "Unless, of course, we find the gold. And then, after expenses, we'll divide up the profit."

So, these are the facts. And now my friends were begging me to get in the water with them.

"Come on Wally—hurry up!"

With another sigh, I shut Ol' Betsy down and put on my mask, air tank, and swim fins. It was now or never (although the never part still sounded like a better deal). I waddled to the ladder and carefully started down.

Ker-slap, Ker-slap, Ker-slap . . .

That was my swim fins slapping against the steel rungs of the ladder as I carefully worked my way down toward the water.

Ker-slap, Ker-slap, "WHOA!" . . . *KER-SPLASH!*

That, of course, was me losing my balance and falling head over heels into the water.

Unfortunately, when I hit, I made the mistake of leaving my mouth open, which meant I swallowed about half of the ocean. I bobbed to the surface coughing and gagging my guts out. "Why did I ever . . . *COUGH, COUGH* . . . let you . . . *GAG, GAG* . . . talk me into this?" I shouted to Wall Street.

"For the gold!" she grinned. "If we ever find that submarine and its buried treasure, we'll be rich . . . filthy, stinking, hire-somebody-else-to-do-our-homework-'cause-we'll-be-too-busy-shopping rich!" Good ol' Wall Street. One thing you can say about her, she loves money.

I turned to Opera. He doesn't have one love, but two. The first is classical music. Everywhere he goes he listens to it on his Walkman—at home, at school, in bed. It's like the earphones are surgically implanted into his head. In fact, I was a little surprised he wasn't wearing them here in the ocean.

Opera's other love is junk food. It makes no difference what it is, as long as it is fried in grease, covered in salt, and goes *CRUNCH* when you bite into it. At one point his mom tried to get him to lose weight by drinking those diet milkshakes made from a powdered mix. The only problem was, when she wasn't looking, he'd get out the frying pan, pour in the salt and grease, and fry the thick shakes like pancakes.

Somehow munching on French-fried Ultra-Skinny defeated the whole purpose.

"You kids be careful."

We looked back at *The Bulwinkle*. That was the name of our boat. Captain Ray was shouting down to us from the pilot house. "The fathometer shows some large movement directly below us, so stay close to the boat."

"You think it's sharks?" Opera called.

"I doubt it."

"What about that sea serpent or monster or whatever it is the guys spotted last night?" I asked.

Uncle Ray shrugged. "Just stay close," he warned.

"Will do," Opera shouted.

Floating there in the water, I wasn't crazy about sharing my swim with man-eating sharks, sea monsters, or floating dead men. "Have we had enough fun yet?" I asked. "Can we get out now?"

"We just got in," Wall Street chided.

"I know, but I'd hate to use up all our fun now and not have any left over for—" Suddenly, I froze. Something brushed against my leg. I spun around to Opera. "Okay, very funny. Knock it off."

Opera looked at me, perplexed. "What?"

"You know what," I said. Then I felt it again. This time it grabbed my swim fin and gave a little pull. I looked down just in time to see a dark shadow swim past and disappear. I wanted to open my mouth and scream, but when you're busy hyperventilating and having a heart attack, sometimes you forget little details like that.

"Wally, what's wrong?" Wall Street asked.

I could only point to the water while doing my best wheezing and gasping routine. Wall Street and Opera exchanged glances, then poked their heads under the water to see.

I did the same. Not because I doubted what I felt, but because I figured if you're going to die, you better know the details . . . just in case you have to fill out forms and stuff when you get to heaven.

I put my head under the water and immediately saw them. Not one but two! Two dark shadows. Obviously sharks. They were racing toward me from below at about a gazillion miles an hour.

For the briefest second I asked myself, *Why am I dying?* And then I remembered what Wall Street had said, "for the gold." Ah, yes, if you're going to die, it might as well be for a good cause.

Chapter 2
We've Got Company!

The way the sharks raced toward us, it was pretty obvious they were in the mood for lunch. And by the way they zeroed in on me, it looked like they'd already picked out their main course. But then, just when I was about to become a McDoogle Big Mac, I saw they weren't sharks at all.

They were dolphins—a big one and a little one.

They zipped by so fast and I was so surprised that I sucked in my breath. (Not a great idea when your head's underwater.) Once again I began my coughing and gagging routine. When I finally finished, I looked up to see the two creatures, about a dozen yards away, jumping and playing at the surface.

Wall Street laughed. "Are they cute, or what?"

"It looks like a mother and a baby," Opera shouted.

A moment later, the dolphins dove under the water. We stuck our heads back underneath and watched. They were definitely playing. It was so cool, the way they rolled and dove and circled each other.

Suddenly, the baby turned and started toward me again. His long, pointed snout was aimed directly at me. *Uh-oh,* I thought. *This doesn't look good.* Closer and closer he came. *Great, I travel all this way just to become some baby dolphin's shish-kebab.* But, then, at the very last second, he veered down and took a playful nip at my swim fin.

Opera began laughing. "He's playing with you!" he shouted. "He's playing tag with your fins."

The little fellow zoomed back to his mom, and they started the whole rolling and diving and circling routine again. I couldn't help smiling.

"See if you can call him," Opera shouted.

"What?"

"See if he'll come when you call."

"How?" I asked.

"How should I know?"

Good old Opera always had an answer for everything. But he was right; the baby did seem to like me. Maybe I could get him to come again. I held out my hand and started snapping my fingers. "Here boy, come here boy, come on fellow."

"He's not a dog," Wall Street said with a laugh. "He's a dolphin. Talk to him in dolphin talk."

"What's that?"

"You've seen those old Flipper reruns. Talk to him like Flipper."

I watched as the baby did another spin and started toward me. Once again he raced directly at me, then dipped down, nipped at my swim fin, and took off.

"Try it," Wall Street urged. "Try talking to him like Flipper. You know, with all those clicking and squeaking sounds."

I glanced around a little nervously. I wasn't used to making a fool of myself (at least not in public). But since Opera and Wall Street were the only ones around, and since we were all fellow Dorkoids, I gave it a shot. I put my hands to my mouth and started the world's sickest and weirdest dolphin call.

"CLICK-CLICK SQUEAL SQUAWK-SQUAWK SQUEAL-SQUEAL CLICK!"

It was awful. I sounded more like a parakeet caught in the spin cycle of a washing machine than a dolphin. In fact, it was so bad that Momma and Babe Dolphin stopped dead in their tracks and just stared at me.

I paused and gave them a little smile.

"Keep it up," Opera said with a laugh. "You must be saying something they understand."

"I just hope it's nothing dirty," I said.

With confidence slowly rising, I continued my dolphin routine:

"CLICK-CLICK SQUEAL SQUAWK-SQUAWK SQUEAL-SQUEAL CLICK!"

The dolphins continued to stare.

Louder and louder, I called:

"CLICK-CLICK SQUEAL SQUAWK-SQUAWK SQUEAL-SQUEAL CLICK!"

"CLICK-CLICK SQUEAL SQUAWK-SQUAWK SQUEAL-SQUEAL CLICK!"

Until I finally got my answer:

"HA-HA! HO-HO! HE-HE!"

At first I thought it was the dolphins. Then I realized it was coming from behind me. Slowly, I turned toward the boat. And there, lined up on the deck, were all four crew members of *The Bulwinkle*. They were leaning on the rail, shaking their heads, and having the laugh of their lives.

My ears turned bright red, and my face burned. My only comfort was knowing that once again I had brought a little joy and merriment into an otherwise bleak and boring world.

* * * * *

Later that afternoon, Opera and I sat on our bunks down in the tiny crew quarters. Once again the ocean was getting a little choppy, and once again I was getting more than a little sick. It had become a routine. Every day at this time, when the waves started heaving and pitching . . . so did I. In fact, I was so predictable, some crew members came down into the cabin and set their watches by me.

Opera was listening to his Walkman. Something by one of those H guys. You know, Handel, Haydn, Hanukkah—someone like that. Anyway, he was also tearing into his fifth bag of salt-covered, deep-fried, grease-saturated chips (with a little potato thrown in the middle). Needless to say, the smell didn't help my stomach much.

"Hey, Wally!" he shouted over his music. "Are you *(MUNCH, MUNCH, MUNCH)* okay?"

"Yeah," I said, trying to swallow back the nausea.

"What?" he shouted.

"Yeah!" I shouted back. It was an obvious lie; I was getting worse by the second.

"Here *(MUNCH, MUNCH, MUNCH)*, have some chips!" Before I could stop him, he shoved the entire bag under my nose. That was all it took. I tried pushing the bag away, but good, kindhearted, always-willing-to-share Opera kept holding it in my face. I opened my mouth to explain the problem, but only succeeded in throwing up into the bag.

"Oooohh! Gross!" he cried.

I gave a sheepish shrug and tried to apologize, but only succeeded in doing a repeat performance.

"Double gross!" Opera shouted.

"Sorry," I muttered.

He closed up the bag, tossed it in the trash, and reached for another. "That's okay, I've got plenty more."

"Wonderful," I groaned, "so do I. . . ."

Suddenly, Eric, a tall, friendly guy who operated the minisub we had on board, poked his head inside. "Hey, Wally, what time do—" he stopped as I finished wiping off my mouth. "Oh, I see you're already done." He glanced at his watch and reset it. "Looks like I'm running a little late today." He turned and headed back out the door as he said, "Thanks."

"Glad to help," I muttered. I reached for my computer magazine to try to take my mind off of all the rolling and pitching. For the time being, it seemed to do the trick. And that was good, 'cause it also gave me the chance to face my other major challenge in life: how to spend all that gold we were going to find.

Luckily, it was a challenge all of us had risen to. In fact, finding the gold and discussing how we were going to spend it was all anyone ever talked about.

"You think we're getting close?" I asked.

"A *dose?*" Opera shouted as he munched away. His Walkman was going full blast. "What type of *dose?*"

"Not *'dose,'*" I shouted back, "*'close.'* Do you think we're getting *close?*"

"To what?" he yelled.

"To finding the submarine?"

"You heard what Uncle Ray said. *(MUNCH, MUNCH, MUNCH.)* It's around here somewhere. He just needs to find it on the fathometer."

"What a weird place for the guy to hide the gold," I said.

"*Mold?*" Opera shouted, suddenly looking at his chips in concern. "I don't think so."

"Not *'mold,' 'gold,'*" I yelled. "What a weird place for the guy to hide the gold."

Opera nodded. "Uncle Ray says the guy was major Looney Tuncs."

"And they never found his boat, *The Peacock* . . . or his body?"

"*'Karate?'*" Opera shouted.

"No . . . his *'BODY.'* They never found his body?"

"Not only that," he shouted back, "but they never found his body, either."

"And that message," I shouted loud enough so he couldn't get it wrong. "Remember the last thing he radioed?"

Opera nodded as he tore open the next bag of chips. *"BEWARE THE STINGER."*

"What do you suppose he meant, 'Beware the Stinger'? You think he was talking about this monster everybody says is around?"

Opera shrugged and returned to his munching. "Or the sharks," he shouted.

"Or the submarine," I offered.

Opera nodded. "Only sharks and submarines don't have stingers."

I took a deep breath. My nausea was coming back, only this time it was because of the fear. When Opera had first asked Wall Street and me if we wanted to look for sunken treasure, we both jumped at the chance. But now . . . with all the talk of missing bodies, undersea monsters, and mysterious stingers, I wasn't so sure.

Still, there was supposed to be over a million dollars' worth of gold down there. I suppose some things are definitely worth risking life and lunch for.

Suddenly, there was a loud, harsh whistle. We both jumped. It wasn't *The Bulwinkle's* whistle, so we quickly scrambled from our bunks and out onto the deck to see.

Off to our port (that's boat talk for "left") some fifty feet away was an old fishing trawler. By the looks of things, her owner didn't much care about her upkeep. She was filthy, falling apart, and her paint was blistered and peeling worse than my back the time I fell asleep on the beach.

But even in its awful shape, you could still make out the name on the bow (that's more boat talk for "front"). On it was painted *THE SEA WITCH*. How appropriate.

A man stood on the deck above the letters. He was heavyset and as dirty and unkempt as his boat. At the moment he was stuffing his mouth full of tobacco. "Alexander!" he yelled. "Hey, Alexander, I'm talking to you!" Then four or five of his other crewmen appeared at his side. Their lack of concern for their own appearances (not to mention monthly showers) was equally obvious.

"Alexander!"

Gradually, one by one, our own crew came out onto our deck.

"ALEXANDER!"

Finally, Captain Ray stepped from the pilot's house. "Gus Perkins," he said through a forced grin, "how good of you to drop by."

Gus Perkins didn't grin back. "I told you to stay out of this area. That gold is mine. You have no claim to it." He spit his chaw of tobacco into the water to show his contempt. "Leave now, before you and your boys get yourself into more trouble than you bargained for."

"That money belongs to whoever finds it," one of our crew members shouted back.

"Yeah," Eric chimed in from beside me. "You want trouble, Perkins, we'll give you trouble."

It surprised me to hear how good-natured Eric suddenly got so angry. But he wasn't the only one.

"Come over here and say that!" one of their guys shouted back at him. His other buddies joined in.

Our guys shouted back even meaner stuff, and their guys returned the insults. But just when things were about to get out of hand, Captain Ray raised his hand and motioned for our side to be quiet.

When things finally settled down, he spoke. His voice was firm and in control. "Captain Perkins, we have as much right to be here as you."

"We'll see about that!" Perkins said with a sneer. The rest of his crew growled in agreement. Perkins spat one last time and turned to enter his ship.

"Pleasant fellow," I said to Eric.

Eric nodded. "Amazing how greed brings out the best in people."

I looked at him, not really getting the point. He gave me a peculiar smile, rumpled my hair, then turned back into the ship. I watched him leave, having no idea how true his comments would become.

* * * * *

Twenty minutes later Wall Street entered Opera's and my cabin. "Hi, guys," she said. She was holding a pencil and a calculator.

Uh-oh. I don't know what it is, but you give Wall Street a pencil and a calculator and she always winds up with *your* money in *her* pocket.

"I've been doing some figuring," she said.

I glanced at Opera nervously. *Here it comes.*

"Since I'm, like, the only female on board, then when the gold is found and divided up, I should get 50 percent."

"What?" Opera and I shouted in unison.

"It's a known fact that women make up 50 percent of the human population. And since I'm the sole representative of that segment, I should be given my fair share."

I looked at Opera. He cleared his throat. "But there's a total of eight people on this boat. The captain, his crew, and us."

"That's right."

"So, at the very most, you should only get one-eighth."

Wall Street scowled. But it wasn't your normal, everyday scowl. It was her world-famous "It's-going-to-take-eleven-bulldozers-and-fifty-cases-of-dynamite-to-make-me-change-my-position" kind of scowl.

Opera tried to change the subject. "If you ask me, I think we're all getting a little carried away with this money and riches stuff."

"What do you mean?" I asked.

"You saw what went on topside just now. They were fighting like cats and dogs and we hadn't even found anything yet."

Wall Street asked, "What's that got to do with—"

"It's even happening to us," he interrupted. "I mean, we were invited out here to have fun. But ever since we got on board, all we do is talk about how we're going to spend our money. Wally with his computers, me with my CDs, and you," he said, turning to Wall Street, "you with your . . ."

She helped him out. "Municipal bonds and stock-option portfolios."

He nodded. "It's like everybody's slowly going crazy."

Wall Street and I exchanged glances. "You're the one that's crazy," Wall Street finally said. "Which one of us doesn't want to be rich?"

"That's right," I agreed.

Opera just sat there.

"You better cut back on your junk food," I offered. "It's starting to affect your thinking."

We all chuckled. But even then something inside me said Opera might have a point. It seemed like everyone was getting a little too greedy, a little too crazy—the crew, Gus Perkins, even ourselves. What was it Pastor Bergman always quoted, "the love of money is the root of all evil"? Well, if that love was the root, it looked like we might be growing ourselves a pretty healthy tree.

Chapter 3

Discovery

When last we left our buglike little buddy, he was buzzing out of his Gnat Cave in his Gnat Mobile to save the world. After all, it is Thursday, and Thursdays are his day for world-saving. Monday it's piano lessons, Tuesday it's cleaning the cat box, Wednesday it's helping little old ladies across the street. That, of course, leaves Thursday for saving the world. (He usually saves Friday for his manicure and lunching with the president.)

Anyway, somewhere out there, the not-so-nice Proverb Guy is stealing all of the world's excuses with his deadly Excuse-a-tron. It is a vile, sinister plot, forcing all of us to do what we say we'll do, instead of making up excuses why we can't. (You don't get much more vile and sinister than that.)

No one's sure what made Proverb Guy such a fiendish fiend. Some say his mother simply bought him underwear that was too tight. Others say it came from watching too many kung fu movies. Then there's the ever-popular theory that he kept trying to open just one fortune cookie without it breaking and exploding all over the table. And the more he opened, the more fortunes he read...until, after the billionth or so cookie, all he could think of were fortunes and proverbs.

Any way you look at it, the guy was several fries short of a McDonald's Happy Meal.

Suddenly, Gnat Man hears the roar of jet engines. He looks up just in time to see a fly swatter the size of Pittsburgh hovering above him. A voice booms from its loudspeakers.

"Confucius say:
'Man whose cup runneth over should fix plumbing.'"

"Proverb Guy," our hero shouts, "is that you?"

"Judge who wants order in court should bring take-out menu."

Immediately, the giant, jet-powered fly swatter crashes down on the road. But Gnat Man is too fast. He swerves his Gnat Mobile to the left, and the swatter misses him. The fly swatter rises and tries again. Gnat Man darts to the right. Another miss. And then, just when Gnat Man is getting to feel pretty cool, just when he realizes, since he's the hero of this story, nothing can ever kill him or mess up his hair, the ol' swatter strikes again and

KER-SPLAT!

The Gnat Mobile becomes instant bug goo.

But fear not, dear reader. For normal superheroes it would be the end, but not for Gnat Man. Besides, with all of the world's excuses being stolen, he can't rely on some flimsy excuse, like being dead, to stop him from saving the world. In a flash of intelligence (and awfully good luck), Gnat Man crawls out of his wreck. He squeezes through one of the little holes in the fly swatter and hops on top, just as the swatter rises. He hangs on for dear life. Once the swatter has leveled off, he races toward the handle—since, as we all know, the handles always serve as the cockpits for flying fly swatters.

Gnat Man pulls at the cockpit door, but it's locked. Fortunately, this is one of those few occasions where having six arms and hands is an advantage. (It gets real expensive when having to buy gloves—and getting the right arm in the right sleeve of a coat can take all day.) But, for once, it's a plus. Gnat Man is able to use the combined strength of all six arms to yank open the door.

He hops inside and shouts, "Give it up, Proverb Guy!"

Proverb Guy spins around and shouts:

"Man who bite electrical wire
get shocking experience!"

But just as Gnat Man prepares to leap at him, Proverb Guy reaches for his Excuse-a-tron belt and presses the reverse button. Suddenly, our hero is hit with the hundreds of excuses the sinister sicko has already collected.

Gnat Man is overcome. He wants to stop Proverb Guy. He wants to save the world. But suddenly he remembers he should have changed his socks; or that he'll be missing his chiropractor appointment; or since Thursday is a school night, is it really the best day to be saving the world?

All these excuses pour in, overwhelming our little buddy, but there's nothing he can do.

Proverb Guy lets out a sinister laugh.

"Confucius say:
'Giraffe with sore throat worse than centipede with athlete's foot.'"

"Please," Gnat Man gasps, "no more, no more."

Proverb Guy laughs louder and

harder. "You're all mine now, Bug Boy. And there's nothing you can do to stop me."

"I want to," our hero shouts, "but I promised Mom I wouldn't get my new Gnat Cape dirty. No, I mean, I want to, but I forgot to make my bed. No, I mean, I want to, but..."

Great Scott! Will our hero ever be able to overcome those feeble excuses? Will he ever be able to beat Proverb Guy? And, most importantly, will he ever be able to stop the grizzly goon from quoting those awful proverbs?

And then, suddenly, just when you thought I was coming up with an answer—

"WALLY, LOOK OUT!"

I glanced up from Ol' Betsy just in time to see the minisub swing directly over my head. It had been resting in its rack at the stern of the boat. But now the crane was hoisting it across the deck and getting ready to drop it into the water. If I didn't get out of the way, it would be dropping me into the water as well.

I shut down Ol' Betsy and leaped to the side.

As they lowered the minisub into the water for a trial run, I couldn't help thinking it looked like something out of a sci-fi flick. In the front she had two portholes—one up in the top part so the operator could see where he was going, the other in the nose for an observer. Normally, it held about three people, but Eric, the minisub operator, had offered to let all of us kids ride with him.

"Wonderful!" Opera had cried.

"Terrific!" Wall Street had shouted.

"No way," I had muttered. (With my luck if I got into the minisub, it would do its best *Titanic* imitation and immediately sink to the bottom.) It wasn't that I was chicken, it's just that I hated to see my friends die at such young ages. "You go ahead," I had said, "I'll follow you down in my scuba gear."

Now, normally, you're supposed to dive in pairs; the "buddy system," they call it. But since the minisub would be right beside me, and since no one else was available, we figured it would be okay.

So there I was, once again slipping on my scuba tank, mask and flippers. I heard one of the crew members shout, "Hey, everybody, McDoogle's going into the water again." I began to wonder if maybe I should start charging admission.

Once again *Ker-slap, Ker-slap, Ker-slap,* I made my way down the ladder toward the water, and once again *Ker-slap, ker-slap,* "WHOA!" . . . *KER-SPLASH!* I made my usual entrance.

Luckily, nobody saw. Well, nobody except Wall Street, Opera, Eric . . . and everybody else on board *The Bulwinkle.* Apparently, the crew had all shuffled on deck to see the show. I bobbed back to the surface doing my usual coughing and gagging routine. Of course everybody was clapping, and of course I gave them my world-famous McDoogle-the-moron wave.

I waited as Wall Street and Opera climbed onto the minisub and down through the hatch. A moment later Eric closed the cover and started the engine. The minisub gave a high whine as air bubbles surrounded her and she started to sink. I dove under the water and followed.

It was a completely different world under there. So peaceful, so calm. There were no sounds except for my breathing and the distant whine of the minisub. The water was crystal clear. I could see Opera and Wall Street, over twenty feet away, waving to me through the mini-sub's windows. Yes sir, everything was incredibly beautiful, which, of course, made me incredibly sad. Not because it was incredibly beautiful, but because I was there, which meant its incredible beauty might soon turn into incredible disaster.

As the minisub continued to sink, I continued to kick and follow her down. Suddenly, there was a dark form to my left. *Uh-oh,* I thought, *here it comes—the ever-popular McDoogle Catastrophe.*

But it wasn't a catastrophe at all . . . it was Momma Dolphin and Babe. I don't know where they came from, but suddenly they appeared and started twirling and circling around me just like yesterday. Once again Babe darted in and poked at my flippers. I reached out, and he shot away. A moment later he was back. Again I reached out. And again he took off. But the third time he stayed just long enough to let me actually touch him.

WOW! His skin was all slick and rubbery . . . just like an old inner tube—or my little sister's scrambled eggs. Take your pick.

He took off but returned again. It was like he was playing a shy little game of tag. His fear slowly faded as he stayed beside me longer and longer. Of course, Momma was always nearby, keeping a careful eye on things. I couldn't blame her. I'm sure my reputation for disaster had also spread throughout the sea world.

Finally, Babe stayed long enough to let me

run my hand over his back, all the way to his top fin. When I touched it, he didn't flinch. It was almost like that's what he had wanted me to do. Then, ever so carefully, he began to flip his tail back and forth. I held the fin tighter. We started to move. It was so cool. He was actually pulling me through the water. I didn't have to kick or do anything. Just hang on.

We began to turn and spin as he picked up speed. I don't know how long we went on like that—maybe five, ten minutes. I'm not sure. All I know is, when I looked over my shoulder to make sure Wall Street and Opera were getting good and jealous, I saw that the minisub was gone. Not gone like it's-just-out-of-sight gone, but gone like Uh-oh, I'm-down-here-all-alone-in-the-deep-blue-sea gone.

I figured now was as good a time as any to have a panic attack. But just before I launched into hyperfear, I saw it. A long, dark, shadowy form. It was about thirty feet below me. Half of it rested on an undersea ledge. The other half stuck out over the ledge with nothing below it but water, water, and more water. There was no bottom in sight—just total blackness. I don't want to say the drop-off went on forever, but if I ever wanted to get some authentic Chinese food, I knew where to go.

I looked back at the long, dark, shadowy form. But this was no ordinary long, dark, shadowy form. No way. This definitely had the shape of a submarine. An old, World War II, got-more-gold-than-we-can-spend-hidden-somewhere-inside-it submarine!

I was so excited that I let go of Babe Dolphin and started swimming straight down toward the wreck. But I didn't get far. Momma Dolphin had other plans. She shot down in front of me and blocked my path. At first I thought she was playing. But each time I tried to get around her she moved in the way. I'd turn to the left, she'd turn to the left. I'd turn to the right, she'd turn to the right. The ol' gal was purposely stopping me.

Maybe she was warning me about sharks or undersea monsters or pirates or dead thieves or—

Actually, that was enough *ors*. After thinking it through, I realized now was as good a time as any to turn tail and race back to the surface for my life. Not that I was scared or anything like that. But I suddenly remembered I hadn't flossed my teeth that morning . . . or washed out my comb . . . or cleaned my glasses . . . or straightened my shoelaces. . . . (Don't you just love excuses? They really come in handy if you want to keep living.)

Above me I saw the shadow of the boat, floating in the water. Good, I hadn't drifted as far away as I thought. But as soon as I surfaced, went through my usual coughing and gagging routine, and finally looked around, I knew my little adventure wasn't quite over.

The boat beside me was NOT *The Bulwinkle*. It wasn't even the pirate's *Sea Witch*. No, I couldn't be that lucky. This boat was much smaller, and by the looks of things, it had been anchored here for quite a while.

Oh, and one other thing. It had the name *Peacock* scrawled on the side—the name of the missing thief's boat!

Chapter 4

Greed Grows

The way I figured it, I had two choices. I could stay in the water and make like a piece of driftwood—until I got washed up on shore and someone found me and decided to use me as a wall decoration for their new seafood restaurant. Or, I could take my chances going on board and hope Mr. Thief was having a good hair day.

It was a tough choice. But since I hate seafood, I decided to climb on board. I carefully stole up the ladder, just as quietly as one of those Navy Seals in the movies. I was a magnificent example of super-spy heroism. No dripping water, no heavy breathing . . . just the banging of my knees as they knocked together in sheer horror.

I reached the deck and silently checked out the place. It was a small cabin cruiser, and it was a total mess. There were orange peels, loose papers, and bird droppings everywhere. Whoever lived here was definitely not into house cleaning.

Part of me wanted to go back, but part of me wanted to sneak down into the cabin and take a peek. Whoever was there probably had the gold. Who knows, maybe they were getting tired of lugging it all over the place. Maybe they were getting lonely. Maybe they'd like to make some new friends to share it with. (Maybe I still believed Superman could really fly.)

It was a long shot, I know. Unfortunately, I had nothing else to do, and not a whole lot of places to go, so I went for it. Ever so carefully, ever so stealthily, I took a step forward. And then, ever so carefully, ever so stealthily, I *"WHHHHHOOAA!"* stepped on my swim fins and crashed face first onto the deck.

KLUNK!

I stayed down, waiting for the spray of machine-gun fire and hoping my dental records were up-to-date so someone could identify my body. But there was nothing. No shooting. No bullets. Not even any gaping wounds.

As I lay there, I tried to think of any sins I hadn't cleared with God. Only one came to mind. *Dear Lord,* I prayed, *I'm sorry for stuffing the back of my pants full of socks when I knew I was getting spanked. And if you let me live through this, I promise never to do it again.* It wasn't much, but it was the best I could come up with on such short notice. Finally, I stood up and, "WHOOAA"-*KLUNK,* gave a repeat performance of landing on my face.

But again, no one came up on deck. Either they were very shy . . . or very gone . . . or very . . . I pushed the thought out of my mind.

Then I heard it . . . a scratching noise. But it was more than scratching. It almost sounded alive. I held my breath and listened.

Scrape, scrape . . . screech

It was coming from below, down in the cabin. I quickly slipped out of my fins. I'd made enough noise to give up the James Bond routine, so I tried another one . . . the Friendly-Dorkoid-Who-Just-Happened-To-Stumble-Upon-The-Boat-Looking-For-A-Half-alive-Thief routine. "Hello . . . is anybody home?"

I took a few steps closer. Now I was able to see down into the cabin. It was in even worse shape than the deck. But there were no people.

Scrape, scrape . . . screech

It was coming from the bathroom down in the cabin. The door was slightly ajar, but I couldn't see in. I fought off a cold shiver and forced myself to start down the steps. "Hello . . . are you okay? Is everything all right in there?"

Scrape, scrape . . . screech

I reached the bottom. I was three steps away, but it was still too dark to see inside. I continued to keep my one-sided conversation going. "I was just in the neighborhood, you know, and thought I'd stop by and—"

Scrape, scrape . . . screech

I was directly in front of the bathroom now, but I still could not see in. Whoever was in there didn't feel much like talking. Or maybe they couldn't talk. Maybe they needed my help. With a deep breath, and another deal with God . . . *If you let me live through this, I promise to stop popping my gum in Sunday school . . .* I stepped forward and pushed open the door.

S C R E E C H ! C A A A W !

I was met with a flurry of feathers.

"AUGHHH!" I cried.

"SCREECH-SCREECH," the feathered thing screamed.

"AUGHHHHHHHH!" I cried even louder.

And then, just when we finally started to have a meaningful conversation, just when we were getting to really know each other, the giant sea gull flapped past my face and out of the bathroom.

I leaned against the door gasping for breath, trying to decide whether to have a heart attack or just a good old-fashioned stroke. That's when I spotted *The Bulwinkle* speeding toward me. Great! I could use a little company.

But just before I clamored back up the steps and onto the deck to wave to them, something else in the bathroom caught my eye. It was on the mirror. I pushed open the door a little further to see. It was scrawled with soap in big letters:

BEWARE THE STINGER

It was the same warning the thief had radioed—the last message he had transmitted before disappearing.

* * * * *

For the next hour everyone on board *The Bulwinkle* was busy dropping anchor, prepping their gear, and getting ready to send down the minisub and a couple of divers. Captain Raymond had thoroughly checked out *The Peacock*. There was definitely no thief on board and definitely no more clues to be found. But that's okay. Our biggest clue was directly below us. The sunken sub was resting on that steep ledge, with all that gold hidden somewhere in it.

I sat inside Eric's minisub, watching as he closed the hatch on us. *CLANK* . . . I swallowed hard as he spun the handle around to seal us in. I don't want to say I was feeling claustrophobic or anything, but suddenly I could relate to those big dill pickles crammed into those tiny glass jars at the supermarket.

Opera, being the thoughtful guy he is, insisted we could all squeeze in. I tried to pass, but he made such a big deal about it that sheer embarrassment forced me to join them. What a sweetheart. If we ever got back alive I'd have to give him something to express my appreciation. You know, something that goes tick-tock when you get it and BOOM-BOOM when you open it.

Eric climbed into his control chair above us. He buckled himself in, hit a few switches, and suddenly we were surrounded by bubbles.

"Wow," I said, looking out the observation porthole and momentarily forgetting my fear. "This is just like Disneyland."

Wall Street, who was sitting on my right, grinned. "Except for the undersea monster, the pirates, and the distinct possibility of losing our lives."

Good ol' Wall Street. I'd have to find something to express my appreciation to her as well.

As the bubbles cleared, we could see Momma and Babe off to port. They were doing their usual diving and spinning routine.

"Beautiful, aren't they?" Eric called down to us.

"I'll say," I answered.

"Dolphins are supposed to be good luck," he said. "There's all sorts of legends about how they save divers' lives."

Suddenly, out of the blue, Wall Street changed the subject. "I think Wally should get a bigger bonus than the rest of us."

"Why's that?" Eric asked, his eyes glued to the controls.

"He's the one who found the gold," she said, "so he should get more money."

I shot her a look. What was she up to? Making sure others got more money than she did was definitely not Wall Street's style.

Eric continued staring at the controls as he answered. "We've all agreed upon the terms, Wall Street. Believe me, if we find this gold, you'll all have more money than you'll know what to do—"

"But *Wally's* the one who found the sub," she interrupted. "He should get the most."

I couldn't believe my ears. Normally, she was the one scrounging for the nickels and dimes and major stock options. Why was she trying to help me?

"And as his agent," she continued, "I, of course, would be getting an extra 30 percent."

Suddenly, things were much clearer.

"Look!" Opera pointed through the porthole. There it was. We could clearly see the barnacle-and-coral-covered hull of the old sub. It was pinkish-white and green, just like the surrounding rocks. In fact, if it wasn't for its long, pointy shape, you'd think it was a rock. The whole thing rested precariously with its nose hanging out over the ledge. It wouldn't take much to send it falling over that ledge into the bottomless pit below—just a major earthquake, or a brief visit by someone world-renowned for his clumsiness. (Another reason I wanted to stay topside.)

"For something this old," Eric said, "she's incredibly preserved."

"What's that dark thing in the middle?" I asked.

"Looks like a giant hole. We'll be working our way toward it," he said.

The two divers appeared on either side of us and moved ahead to explore. A moment later we had all arrived at the tail section of the sunken sub.

Eric pressed the intercom button and spoke. "We're at the aft section now, Captain."

"Roger," came the voice through the overhead speaker. "Not to push you boys, but move as quickly as you can. Things are getting a little choppy up here. We might have the makings of a storm."

"Roger," Eric answered. He flashed his headlights off and on at the divers. It was a signal. They nodded and started moving up the submarine. Carefully, they checked her hull, every nook, every cranny, every hole. Sometimes with their hands, sometimes their heads, sometimes with their entire body.

"Fools," Eric muttered.

"What's that?" I asked.

He motioned toward the divers. "They have no idea what could be lurking in those openings—moray eels, stingrays, you name it. They could lose their hand, their arms. Shoot, they could lose their life," he said, snapping his fingers, "just like that."

"So why are they doing it?" I asked.

"The same reason you checked out *The Peacock* on your own," he answered.

"You mean, to find the gold?"

He flashed me a sly grin. "Bingo."

There was something about the way he smiled that made me nervous. Maybe it wasn't the smile; maybe it was what he said. The fact that normal, sane men were risking their lives to make a couple of extra bucks seemed kinda spooky.

But just as scary was the fact that nobody tried to stop them. It was like the gold had somehow become more important than their lives. Yes sir, ol' greed was definitely making headway in our little brains. And the closer we got to the gold, the more it took control.

The overhead speaker came to life again. "Eric . . ."

"Yes, Captain."

"We've got ourselves a situation up here."

"The storm?"

"Negative. Captain Perkins just radioed."

"And?"

"He spotted us beside *The Peacock*. He knows we've found the sub, and he's coming to board us."

"He's what?"

"His men are armed, and they're coming to board us."

"They can't do that!" Eric practically shouted into his microphone. "That's piracy!"

"Roger. Surface as fast as you can. Things may get a little sticky up here. I'm going to need all the manpower I have."

"On our way, Captain."

Eric flashed his lights at the divers and motioned for them to surface.

Wall Street, Opera, and I exchanged frightened glances. I felt a cold knot growing in my stomach. Don't get me wrong, I was all for defending *The Bulwinkle* and our gold. I was just concerned about my allergies. Especially the ones involving hot lead. It seems I break out in a bad case of pain whenever bullets enter my body.

But there was something even more sinister. Something none of us had noticed was lurking around the gaping hole in the middle of the submarine . . . something big, dark, and creepy that had been hiding in the shadows, preparing to meet us.

Lucky for it, we'd be back. *Unlucky* for us, it would be waiting. . . .

Chapter 5

Pirate Trouble

It was a race to see who would reach *The Bulwinkle* the fastest—our minisub or *The Sea Witch*. Fortunately, the minisub won. Unfortunately, Wall Street, Opera, and I were quickly escorted down to our quarters and told to stay there until things cooled off. That, of course, meant we were going to miss out on all the cool shouting and fighting and bleeding. (I tell you, sometimes being a kid really has its drawbacks.)

So there we were, locked in our quarters, waiting calmly and maturely for the outcome. Well, if you call crouching on our hands and knees with our ears pressed against the door to listen "calm and mature."

We heard angry voices when *The Sea Witch* first arrived. But that was half an hour ago. Since then, we hadn't heard a thing. Not a single sword clang, exploding cannon, or rifle blast. Nothing.

"This is the lamest pirate invasion I've ever been a part of," Wall Street said with a sigh.

"Yeah," Opera complained. "I at least expected some hooting and hollering or . . ."

"Or singing," Wall Street continued, "like in *Pirates of the Caribbean.*"

"Yeah," Opera nodded. "That would have been neat."

At last I heard something. "What was that?" I asked.

"I didn't hear any—"

"Shhh . . ." I said. "It's a type of rumbling. Can't you hear it?"

We leaned with our ears to the door, straining to listen.

"There it is again."

This time it was louder. A low rumbling, like thunder, only louder and more ominous.

"Maybe they're having a bowling tournament," Wall Street guessed.

"Either that or they're rolling the dead bodies off into the water," I suggested.

"Uh . . . guys . . ." Opera tried to get our attention, but it was too late. Our imaginations had already kicked into overtime.

"Or maybe they're rolling powder kegs onto the ship to blow it up!" Wall Street chimed.

"Uh, guys . . ."

"Or tanks."

"Yeah, they're bringing on a whole army of tanks to—"

"Or bombs. Nuclear bombs to blow us into tiny, glow-in-the-dark, kiddie confetti!"

"Or—"

"GUYS!"

"What??" we shouted back in annoyance.

"It's not the pirates," Opera said. "It's me. It's my stomach."

Wall Street and I both glared at him.

He gave a little shrug. "It's been an hour since I had any junk food; what do you expect?"

He had a point. What could we expect? It wasn't Opera's fault he was addicted. Alcoholics have their booze. Druggies have their drugs. Opera has his munchies.

But, like all junk food junkies, Opera had his secret stash. Proudly, he lifted up his shirt to reveal two bags of extra crispy chips taped around his waist. Next, he reached into his baggy socks and pulled out two cans of clam dip.

Good ol' Opera, always prepared.

Of course, his folks had tried everything they could to break him of his junk-food habit:

—Rehabilitation clinics, where they told him that boiled broccoli tasted just like potato chips. (It might have worked if they'd gotten rid of the green color . . . and if Opera had the IQ of a rock.)

—A 12-step recovery program where they made him face his problem head-on . . . "Hi, my name's Opera and I'm a Munchoholic."

—Then, of course, there were the shock therapy sessions where they gave him electrical shocks every time he ate a chip . . . until the Department of Energy shut them down for using up too much electricity.

No matter what they did, nothing worked.

He tore into the first bag of chips and started to crunch away. I knew it would be hopeless to try to hear anything through the door. Nothing is louder than salt-saturated munching—unless you count the sighs of ecstasy from the muncher.

I rose and crossed back to my bunk. It was time to pull out Ol' Betsy and return to my Gnat Man story. With any luck I'd get it finished before the pirates broke down the door with their swords and turned us into kid-kebabs.

When we last left Gnat Man, he was inside Proverb Guy's flying fly swat-

ter. The proverbial punster had just
turned his Excuse-a-tron on our hero,
spraying him with every imaginable
excuse under the sun. And now, instead
of trying to destroy the machine, Gnat
Man can only come up with excuses.

"What's the matter?" Proverb Guy
taunts. "Don't you want to save the
world?"

"Yes," our insect hero gasps,
"but...but I got this hangnail. No,
no, I mean, it's Thursday and I'll
miss my favorite TV show. No, I mean,
I'd love to save the world, but I
have to organize my sock drawer."

Proverb Guy lets out a sinister
laugh. "Give it up, Bug Boy, you'll
never run out of excuses!"

"But...but...but..."

In his glee, Proverb Guy feels
another wave of proverbs coming on.

"Confucius say:
'Man who swallow lit candle
have burning indigestion.'"

"No," Gnat Man cries. "No more
proverbs, please!"

"Man who look like million dollars
is green and wrinkled."

Gnat Man drops to his knees (all six
of them). "Stop it, please, I can't
take any more! Please, stop!"
But Proverb Guy shows no mercy.

"Chicken who crosses street,
still slightly undercooked."

"AUGH!" our hero cries. "I can't
take any more, I can't——"
And then, just when Gnat Man is
about to die from bad jokes, Proverb
Guy suddenly starts scratching. That's
right. First his left wrist, then his
right, then his neck, then under the
waistband of his Fruit of the Looms.
"What's wrong?" our hero shouts.
"I itch!" Proverb Guy cries. "Everywhere!" He rips off his shirt. "Listen,
would you mind scratching between my
shoulder blades there?"
Being one of the nicer nice guys,
Gnat Man obliges.
"A little to the left...and down."
But before our heroically handsome

hero is too helpfully helpful, he has a hunch (say that seven times fast). "Flea Boy!" he shouts. "Is that you? Are you here, you little mite?"

"That's right," a tiny voice squeaks from somewhere under Proverb Guy's left armpit. "It's me, your favorite sidetick, ready, willing, and pretty hungry."

"Ow!" Proverb Guy screams as he slaps under his arm. "Get him off! Get him off!"

Gnat Man wants to help. But try as he might, our good guy can only come up with more excuses. "I'm sorry," he shouts, "but I'm still under the power of your Excuse-a-tron. I want to help. But I've got to brush the dog...I mean, rake the leaves...I mean, take out the trash...er, uh, clean up my——"

"All right, all right!" the putrid poet screams. He fumbles for the Excuse-a-tron's switch and snaps it off. The machine winds down. Now, Gnat Man is no longer under its power. Now, he is free of excuses and can save the world.

"Get him off!" Proverb Guy shouts. "Get him off! You promised, you promised!"

Since Gnat Man is in the Superhero union and since it's in their contract to always keep their word, he calls off his little buddy. "Okay, Flea Boy, you can stop now. Thanks for the help."

"No problem," Flea Boy squeaks. "You know how I like to 'bug' bad guys." He gives a tiny little giggle as he hops off Proverb Guy and onto the nearby door handle. "Listen, can you guys drop me off at the nearest pet shop? I'm still a little hungry and could go for some dessert—something along the lines of a poodle's ear would be nice. Or maybe a nice, tender kitten's—"

But before he finishes, Proverb Guy suddenly lunges for the door and throws it open.

"AHHHHHH..." Flea Boy cries as he falls out of the cockpit.

And always remembering his manners, Gnat Man sticks his head out to shout, "Thanks for the help."

"DON'T MENTION ITTTT...."

Gnat Man spins back to Proverb Guy just in time to see him reach for his Excuse-a-tron.

"Now it's just the two of us," the bad guy sneers.

But suddenly, before he can snap on the switch—

"Okay, kids, you can come topside now."

I looked up from Ol' Betsy to see Eric sticking his head into the cabin.

"So, is it safe?" Wall Street asked.

"Yeah." Opera chimed in. "Did you get rid of all the pirates, and can we get our gold now?"

"Not exactly," Eric said with a sigh.

"Why? What's up?" I asked.

"You better come with me. The crew's having a meeting and you should be part of it."

Opera, Wall Street, and I exchanged nervous glances. I put away Ol' Betsy, and we headed for the door.

Chapter 6

A Time for Action

"You can't be serious!" Eric demanded.

Captain Ray gave him a hard look and repeated himself quietly and evenly. "We will mark the sub's location and return to the harbor until the storm passes. There we will begin negotiating with *The Sea Witch* on how to split the money."

"*Split* the money?" another crew member complained.

"I'm afraid so," Captain Ray said.

"But we found it first," Opera whined.

"I know . . . and by rights, it should be ours. But sometimes you have to make compromises."

"It's not fair," another crew member said

"He's right," Eric agreed. "We're so close. The minisub's still in the water. Let me make one last dive."

Captain Ray gave a heavy sigh. "It's better this way. We'll have less trouble if we cooperate."

"Cooperate! With those pirates!" Eric scoffed.

"That's going to cut our take down 50 percent," another crew member protested.

You could tell everybody was pretty steamed. Who could blame them? We had worked so hard and so long to find the gold. And now we were going to have to split it, just because some bully pirates threatened to turn our faces into pizza topping. I could feel my own face grow hot with anger as I realized my wealth was about to be cut in half.

"I'm sorry, fellows," the Captain said, looking around the table. "But this is the safest and smartest thing to do."

A heavy silence hung over the group. It made no difference that Captain Ray had probably saved all our lives by making a deal with *The Sea Witch* captain. The only thing that seemed to count was that we were going to lose some of our gold.

"I say we take a vote," Eric said.

Others around the table agreed. "Yeah . . . it's our necks . . . let us decide if we want to take the risk!" Things were getting pretty loud until Captain Ray raised his hands. Everyone quieted down.

"This is not a democracy," he said quietly.

"As your captain, I have to make the decision. And I have made it."

You could tell no one was thrilled about his decision. But, like he said, he was the captain. He turned to Eric. "Let's pull the minisub out of the water and get her stowed. With any luck we'll make it to the harbor before nightfall."

"But Captain Ray," Eric started to protest.

"Those are my orders, Eric. Let's get started."

With that the captain rose to his feet—a clear signal to the rest of the crew that the meeting was over. Slowly, reluctantly, the others got up. There was lots to do before we could raise anchor and leave.

I stepped outside the pilot house and waited for Eric. The storm was getting closer. That meant the sea was getting choppier by the minute—and my stomach was getting queasier by the second. A quarter of a mile away, *The Sea Witch* sat anchored—no doubt making sure we would hold to our word like Captain Ray had promised.

When Eric stepped out, I was immediately at his side. Thanks to the approaching storm, the deck was doing a lot of rocking. That, of course, meant I was doing a lot of stumbling and staggering. Still, I managed to stay on my feet and asked, "What would it hurt if—"

"OAF!" (That was me crashing into the side rail.)

"I mean, if we were just to make one more little dive?"

"WHOAAAAA . . ." I staggered the opposite direction until I hit the steel wall of the pilot house.

CLANG

Eric paid no attention. "You heard the Captain," he said as he continued walking and I continued my pinball machine imitation.

"Yeah, but—*WHOAAAA . . ."* (More staggering, topped off by a nice hard fall on the deck.)

BANG!

I started rolling toward the edge and would have fallen overboard if Eric hadn't reached down and pulled me to my feet.

"Stop fooling around," he said. "I want that gold as much as you, but you have to remember, the Captain's the captain. Whatever he says goes."

"Yeah, but—"

"There's no way I can disobey him." He hesitated a second. "Unless . . ."

"Unless what?"

"Never mind." He let me go and headed toward the minisub.

Once again I staggered and fell. After a few

more *"OAF"*s, *"WHOA"*s, *CLANG*s (and a *"YEEOW THAT SMARTS!"* thrown in just to break the monotony), I managed to catch up to Eric and ask him what he meant. "Unless what?" I repeated.

He slowed to a stop and lowered his voice. "I have to obey the Captain." He glanced around and continued. "But if some kid were to disobey, maybe do a little diving on his own . . ."

"Yeah . . ."

"And I had to take the minisub down to rescue him . . ."

"Yeah . . ."

"And I just happen to swing by the sunken sub one last time on the way up . . ."

"That's a perfect idea!" I cried. "So who do you have in mind?"

He looked at me and started to smile.

I looked at him and started to sweat.

* * * * *

It was a little tricky staggering and bouncing along the deck without drawing too much attention. So was sneaking into the gear room to get my tank, mask, and flippers. But everyone was pretty busy getting ready to leave, so they didn't seem to mind my afternoon workout of bouncing from rail to wall and wall to rail. At last I made it to the diving ladder with my gear.

And then, after the ol' familiar *Ker-slap, Ker-slap, "WHOA!"* . . . *KER-SPLASH!* I was back in the water.

The nice thing about being under the water instead of on top is you don't notice the little things . . . like the rocking and rolling of the ship (and your stomach), or the screaming and hollering of everybody at you for jumping in.

I'm sure someone was already shouting, "McDoogle overboard! McDoogle overboard!" but it didn't matter because I didn't hear them. All I heard was the quiet, peaceful silence of my own breathing, and my air bubbles as they gurgled past my ears.

My air tank was full, which meant I could stay down about twenty minutes. No problem. Any second Eric would hop in that minisub of his and come to my "rescue." Of course, when I got back, Captain Ray would have a fit and confine me to quarters for the rest of my life. No problem. I'd rather be confined to quarters for the rest of my life with a million dollars than be totally free and flat broke.

I floated about ten feet below the surface waiting for Eric to climb into his minisub and get going. But he was taking forever. It was about then that an idea came to mind:

Why not go down and try to find the gold on my own?

Of course, there were a thousand reasons not to go, like:

—all the creatures hiding inside waiting to bite my hands off,
—the imaginary or not so imaginary monster guarding it,
—the warning: "Beware the Stinger,"
—and let's not forget the basic but ever-popular drowning.

All that against one and only one reason to go:

GREED!

Ah, yes, that magical little word. That one word that carried more power than all the other words combined. That one word that turned all the other risks into small potatoes.

I glanced around me. This time there was no Momma or Babe to block me. No captain within hearing distance to forbid me. No pirates to stop me. Perfect. It was just me and the submarine.

I'd seen it from the surface. I'd seen it through the minisub's window. But I'd never seen it in person.

I looked down at the wreck. There it lay, begging me to visit. I took a deep breath, readjusted my mask, and started for it. Chances were high that I would find the gold and become everybody's hero.

Well, maybe those are the chances for normal people, but let's not forget who we're dealing with here. . . .

Chapter 7

Anybody Home?

I continued down toward the wreck. As the water pressure built up, I had to clear my ears. It's kinda like when you go up a mountain, how you have to keep yawning and blowing.

I looked up again at the minisub. For some strange reason it was still floating in the water next to *The Bulwinkle*. Its engine was still silent.

And then, finally, I reached the wreck.

I stretched out my hand and touched the hull. It felt exactly like it looked—all barnacles and coral-like. In fact, it was hard to believe there was actually something smooth and man-made underneath.

I remembered what Eric had said about animals hiding in the holes, so I pulled back and floated two or three feet above the thing. Don't get me wrong. I was all for finding the money and being a hero—I just wasn't crazy about being a dead hero. Finding a million dollars in gold would be great—getting it past the security guards in heaven might be a little tricky.

I swam forward, slowly moving along the hull. Everywhere I looked there were coral, barnacles, and waving plants with lots of fish darting in and around. What a place. But other than your normal, heart-stopping splendor, everything else was pretty much the same . . . plenty of beauty, but no booty.

I noticed the large gash up toward the middle. It was big enough for one man (or several monsters) to slip through. I glanced back up at the minisub. With any luck it would be on its way so I wouldn't have to explore the opening. Then again, we've already discussed my luck, haven't we?

Oh well, I thought as I drifted toward the jagged hole, *it won't hurt to take a little peek— just as long as I don't go inside.* Past the opening, there was more than enough darkness and creepy shadows to go around. But as far as I could tell, there was no gold. Nothing, except—

Wait a minute! I thought I saw something. A reflection. I fumbled with the flashlight attached to my belt and somehow managed to snap it on.

There was a blinding glare, an unbearable brightness. At first I thought someone was taking flash pictures, or that they had finally dropped the big one and I was getting nuked. Then I realized I was shining the flashlight in my own eyes. Mustering all of my McDoogle braininess, I turned the flashlight the other direction.

Much better.

The beam cut through the darkness into the wreck, revealing more coral, rock, and plants. Then it caught a reflection at the bottom. It looked like some sort of mirror. I moved in closer until I saw that it wasn't a mirror at all. It was glass—the glass of a diver's mask. A very new diver's mask.

I didn't want to go inside, but I knew I had to. If there was a diver's mask, it meant there had been a diver. And if there had been a diver, chances are this is where he hid the gold.

I inched my way into the wreck, shining the flashlight in every direction at once. I was in no mood for a surprise attack. I had better things to do with my life than become a shark snack or monster munchie.

I drifted deeper and deeper inside. Something in my gut yelled, *Are you crazy!? Turn around!* But I was so close . . . if the thief had been here, so had his gold. And if his face mask had come off, that meant he might have dropped the treasure, right here, right on the floor below me.

Everything inside screamed, *Turn back!* Everything but my greed.

I floated in closer and closer. Still I saw nothing unusual . . . just the little fish guys darting all around . . . and the face mask resting on the floor . . . and, of course, the sea monster rushing at me from the left.

SEA MONSTER!!

I don't know where it came from, but I knew where it was heading. AT ME! The massive blob raced toward me at a zillion miles an hour. I tried to get out of the way, but it did no good. Suddenly, I was covered in rubbery arms and suction cups. I kicked and slapped, but I wasn't sure what I was kicking and slapping at. Then I saw its mouth. It had a beak like a bird's. Rubbery arms, suction cups, a beak like a bird? Immediately, I knew what it was. Either an alien from some distant galaxy . . . or an octopus. And as much as I hoped for an alien, I knew when my autopsy report came out, the adults would insist on something more boring, like an octopus.

But not just any octopus. This baby was the queen mother of 'em all. I remembered Eric mentioning that octopuses liked to hang out in wrecks. I also remember him saying they were harmless, that they were shy and never attacked people.

But ol' Queeny here had obviously missed that part of the lecture. For being shy and peaceful, she was doing a pretty good imitation of being pushy and deadly!

I don't know how long we struggled in that dance of death, but it was obvious she had been taking lessons. And for a monster, she danced pretty well (though I wish she'd have let me lead).

There was no way out. Everywhere I looked there were slithery arms and suction cups. And then I saw it: an eye.

AN EYE? (Is there an echo in here?)

That's right. I'm not sure how many she had, but one was plenty. It was as big as my fist. And, speaking of fists, I had an idea. (Now, if you're into the prevention of cruelty to animals [or sea monsters], you better not read this part.) I had no choice. It was either her or me. It was either my fist in her eye or my body in her stomach. I wiggled my left hand free from her grip, reached high over my head, and swung.

KER-SWISH!

That was me missing her by a mile. I'd forgotten how slowly things move underwater. Queeny had easily ducked out of the way, and I had easily missed.

I tried again.

KER-SWISH!
And again.
KER-SMASH!
Third time's the charm. I slugged her hard in the eye (checking first, of course, to make sure she wasn't wearing glasses). The poor girl got the hint, because she suddenly pushed off and darted away.

So did I.

I kicked and swam for all I was worth. It didn't matter which direction . . . anywhere, to get away from the monster . . . anywhere to be safe. Unfortunately, when the bubbles cleared and I could see, I realized that "anywhere" was deep into the far recesses of the wreck.

I was surrounded by the sub. Everywhere I looked there were walls and ceilings and floor. I was completely turned around. I knew I had come in through the hole. But where was the hole? Behind me? In front of me? Where?

I shined my flashlight back and forth, looking for the way out. There was nothing but a long, narrow passage leading in both directions. My heart pounded as I gasped for breath. At this rate I'd be using up my air way too fast. I had to stay calm. I forced myself to relax, to take slow, deep breaths. And then, just when I was settling down and controlling my breathing, I turned and ran smack-dab, face-to-face (actually face-mask-to-empty-eye-sockets) with . . . a floating corpse.

A FLOATING CORPSE!! (Yes, that's definitely an echo.)

Of course, this meant I had to begin the whole process of screaming, panicking, and getting lost all over again. Only this time I did a lot better (practice makes perfect). I kept bumping and crashing into the walls or ceiling or floor or whatever until boredom finally took over and I decided to try something different . . . like being calm and rational.

I pushed myself against the side wall and waited for the bubbles to clear. And there, less then ten feet away, appeared my old buddy, Floating Corpse. I've got to tell you, I've seen better looking faces. But I guess floating underwater a few weeks isn't so great on the complexion.

There was no doubt in my mind, this had been the owner of the face mask . . . and of the gold. It made perfect sense. No one had ever seen him come back from the dive because he never did come back. Maybe the octopus got him, maybe something worse. Whatever the case, it looked like he had come down to make a major deposit, but wouldn't be making any withdrawals for a long, long time.

Once again I flashed my light in all directions, looking for a way out. I hated to be a party pooper. As much as my old friends, Queeny and Floating Corpse, wanted me to hang around, I remembered Mom insisting that I come back home alive. And since children are supposed to obey their parents, I really didn't have much say in the matter. Like it or not, I had to live.

And then I saw it, just ahead . . . a wall.

A WALL! (Okay, that's enough echoing.)

As I scanned it with my light, I noticed that it wasn't just any wall. This one had four large tubes sticking out of it. Instantly, I knew what they were. Torpedo tubes—the tubes they put torpedoes in when they fire them from submarines. I'd seen things like this in half a dozen old World War II movies. There was no doubt about it. I was at the front end of the sub and those were its torpedo tubes.

One tube still had its hatch closed. The others were open but blocked with coral and barnacles and the usual ocean junk, so you couldn't see through them. Then I noticed the barnacles and plants around the upper left tube had been broken off a little. Not a lot, but enough.

Could it be? My mind raced. I threw a nervous look back at my buddy, Floating Corpse, but he was giving no clues. I looked back at the tube.

Hmmm . . .

Finally, I started toward it. If I were hiding gold in a submarine, wouldn't the perfect place be inside a torpedo tube?

I glanced down to the floor and happened to notice it was moving. That's strange, why on earth is the floor—? And then I realized it wasn't the floor that was moving, it was all the baby octopuses covering the floor.

BABY OCTOPUSES! (Sorry about that echo, but I had to get one more in.)

That's right. Dozens, maybe hundreds of baby octopuses. They were all over the place. No wonder Queeny was so frisky. She was just trying to protect her kids.

I was careful not to step on them as they scurried back and forth across the floor. It was more than a little creepy and I would have turned and swum out of there . . . if it weren't for that torpedo tube.

It was directly in front of me now. I knew I should look in it, maybe even stick my hand inside. It wasn't a thrilling thought, especially when I recalled the warning on the mirror: "Beware the Stinger." What did it mean? As far as I could tell ol' Queeny had no "stinger." And Floating Corpse was certainly stingerless. That kinda narrowed it down to here. Right here, inside the tube. Right here, something was waiting for my unsuspecting hand to reach in and—

Another thought quickly formed. A "stinger" is a weapon, right? I mean, for bees and hornets and things, it's their only defense. I looked back at the tube. And the only defense for submarines back then was their torpedoes.

Could it be . . . ?

Of course! It was a clue the guy had used to say where he was putting the gold. It was right here, right inside the torpedo tube! Right inside the submarine's "stinger"! Now I absolutely *had* to look. There was no getting around it.

I reached up and shined my flashlight inside. There were the usual tiny fish, and rust stuff was all around. But deep inside, almost at the other end, was a bright orange something. . . .

It was a knapsack!

My heart pounded harder. I held the light with my left hand and carefully reached in with my other. But the knapsack was too far inside. I stretched for all I was worth (which, if I got my hands on that sack, would be a heap.) I reached in up to my shoulder, but the knapsack was still too far. It looked like Floating Corpse wanted to make sure it would be in there good and safe. In fact, he'd packed it down so far, I was surprised it didn't come out the other end.

And there was my answer! The other end! I'd go back outside the sub, swim around to the front, and pull the knapsack out the other end!

I glanced at my watch. I'd been under water ten minutes. Half my air was used up. I had to hurry.

I spun around and peered through the darkness of the sub. Somewhere, back there, was the hole I had come through. Floating Corpse continued to hover about ten feet away. I wasn't keen on passing him or about visiting Queeny again. But it was the only way out, the only way to the gold.

I pushed off and began to swim.

Floating Corpse was a little to the left, which meant I stayed a lot to the right. But even then, when I passed, I felt one of his floating hands bump against my shoulder. I shuddered. It was almost like he was trying to say something. Trying to warn me to get out of there and get back to the ship while the getting was good.

But I didn't listen. I figured, in his state, the gold meant nothing. In mine, it meant everything.

Unfortunately, I was about to learn, that "everything" is too high a price to pay for any *thing*. . . .

Chapter 8

Going Down

I swam back through the dark submarine. After a minute or so I saw some light. It was filtering in, very faint, but it was enough for me to know I was heading toward the opening I'd come in. What luck! Imagine me, Wally McDoogle, actually choosing the right direction. Of course, when you only have one direction to choose from, the chances of making a wrong decision are kinda slim. But with my luck, I needed all the help I could get.

The hole slowly came into view, its light growing brighter and brighter. I kept waiting for Queeny to pop out and give me another friendly hug, but she was nowhere in sight.

I reached the opening. Quickly, I shot through it and into the light. Ah, free at last. The minisub was just ahead, obviously searching for me. I could see Wall Street and Opera in the windows.

I guess they'd talked Eric into letting them tag along. That was fine with me. The more witnesses who saw me claim my gold, the better. I also noticed Momma and Babe Dolphin swimming around. Great. The more the merrier.

Eric flashed his lights at me. I'm sure he expected me to turn right around and follow him back to *The Bulwinkle*. But the thought of becoming an instant millionaire had changed my plans slightly. Instead of following him, I waved for him to follow me.

He didn't get it, and he flashed his lights again. Then again.

Meanwhile, Opera was standing at the window making like a traffic cop, waving his arms for me to follow. I shook my head and waved for him to follow. He shook his head harder and waved even bigger. I shook my head even harder and waved even—well, you probably get the picture. The point is, Opera and I may have been doing Dueling Aerobics, but there was no way we were communicating. So, without another word (as if we were doing much talking, anyway), I turned and started for the front of the sunken wreck.

Momma and Babe Dolphin zipped close by me a couple of times. Almost too close. That's okay. I figured they were just trying to warn me about the octopus. I wanted to tell them that I'd already run into their buddy and that we'd worked things out, but my Dolphinese was still a little rusty so I just kept on swimming.

I glanced at my watch. Eight minutes of air left. I had to hurry.

I swam toward the front of the sub. I have to tell you, it looked a lot more inviting on the outside in the light than it had on the inside in the dark.

I glanced down at the ocean floor and saw— Oops. There was no ocean floor. At least not for another million miles or so. I'd forgotten that the wreck rested on a ledge and that the front end was sticking out over a bottomless pit.

A moment later, I spotted the opening to the torpedo tubes. There were two on my side and, I'm sure, just around the nose there were two on the other side. But it was these two, particularly the top right one, that had my interest. It was the one with the orange knapsack, which of course meant it was the one that held all that life-changing, make-you-richer-than-you-can-ever-imagine gold (either that or some kid's very soggy lunch).

I shined my light into the opening. Sure enough, there it was. Just as orange and promising as ever . . . and this time within easy reach. I knocked off the barnacles and coral that were in the way and carefully stuck my hand inside. Slowly, deeper and deeper I reached until . . . there, I felt the nylon strap. I wrapped my hand around it and pulled.

It didn't budge.

I pulled again.

Repeat performance.

The minisub was coming in closer. Eric flashed his lights at me more quickly than ever. Opera waved from the window more comically than ever. And Momma and Babe darted around me more frantically than ever.

Obviously, no one knew what I was doing. Either that or they all knew something I didn't. That last thought made me a little nervous. So far I had made it over three and a half minutes without any major disaster or catastrophe happening. No fumbling, no stumbling, no dying. It just wasn't normal. Something was definitely wrong because everything was so right. Luckily, I wouldn't have to worry much longer. My suspicions would soon be confirmed. . . .

I reached my other arm inside and, with both hands, gave the knapsack my hardest tug yet. It moved, but only a fraction of an inch. Then it dawned on me. The thing wasn't stuck. It was just heavy. Gold is heavy. Real heavy. And a million dollars of it probably weighed a ton. (Too bad this guy didn't steal a million dollars worth of chicken feathers—that would have been a lot easier to move.)

I started to panic. I hadn't come all this way just to find my fortune and leave it. I had to do something. I moved my hands along the knapsack until I felt a buckle. Going strictly by feel, I unfastened it, pulled back the flap, and reached inside. There could have been a hundred animals hiding in it, waiting to take off my hands, but I wasn't thinking about them.

All I was thinking about was the gold.

Then I felt them. Hard, cold bars. Like bricks but a little longer, a little smoother, and a whole lot more expensive. I wrapped my hands around one and pulled. It was surprisingly heavy, but not nearly as heavy as the knapsack. I pulled it out of the sack and drug it out of the tube and into the light.

It was incredible the way it sparkled. It was beautiful. But it wasn't enough.

Having no pockets, I heaved it into my swim trunks and reached for the next bar. It was just as incredible and just as beautiful.

I should have been happy with two. After all, two were practically a life's fortune in themselves. But there's a funny thing about greed. Enough is never enough.

I reached back into the tube. Maybe the knapsack would be lighter now. I pulled on the strap again. It moved, but only a few inches. I had to get a foothold. I had to brace myself against the sub and give it everything I had. I glanced down and saw the other torpedo tube below me. I put my foot in it. There. Now I had some leverage, something I could push against.

Just then, Momma zoomed in and gave me a poke with her nose. But this was no "Tag-you're-it" poke. This was a major "It's-supposed-to-hurt-and-if-you-don't-get-out-of-here-this-sec ond-I'll- break-your-ribs" kind of poke.

"OW!" I yelled, waving at Momma. But of course, she was already gone. I turned back to my yanking.

"UUMPH!" The knapsack moved nearly a foot. All right!

I gave another pull, even harder:

"UUUUMMMMPH!"

It was almost out. One more heave-ho and I'd have her. I saw Momma coming at me again, but this time I was prepared. I waited, and then, at just the right second, I smacked her hard on the nose. She let out a squeal and veered off. I was sorry, but it served her right. This was my gold and nobody was going to stop me from getting it.

I grabbed the strap, braced myself, and gave it everything I had.

"UUUUUUUUMMMMMMMMMPH!"

Finally, the knapsack slid out to the very edge. That was the good news. Unfortunately, every silver lining has its cloud. Or in my case, major storm.

The knapsack was so heavy that its weight caused the whole wreck to shift, to tilt forward. Not a lot, but it had been balanced so precariously, that a little was enough. I heard this loud grating sound and would have been worried, but I had other things on my mind . . . like losing the gold. As the sub tilted forward, the knapsack slipped off the edge of the torpedo tube and started to fall.

"NOOOO!" I screamed as I reached out to catch it.

It wasn't a bad catch. In fact, it was pretty good. The only problem was, the knapsack was so heavy that it immediately yanked me off my feet. I lost my balance and started falling with it.

"AUGH!"

Suddenly, I was met with one of life's little tests. I had basically two choices . . .

A: Hang on to the gold and fall all the way
    to the bottom of the ocean. Or . . .

B: Let go of the gold and grab hold of the
    second torpedo tube I was currently
    falling past.

I hate pop quizzes, don't you? Unfortunately,
I'm never very good at them, so I chose the third
answer, which was . . .

C: All of the above.

That's righ. Even now, my greed wouldn't let
me part with the gold. So, falling past the lower
torpedo tube, I reached out and grabbed it with
my left hand while hanging onto the knapsack
with my right. What a brilliant solution. I hung
there a moment, amazed at my intelligence,
until I noticed another minor problem. For some
reason my handgrip inside the torpedo tube was
moving.

I looked into it and realized I wasn't hanging
onto the tube. I was hanging onto something
    inside the tube. Something big and round
and made of steel. Something big and round
that looked exactly like a torpedo. There was a
good reason for this.

It WAS a torpedo!

Somehow, with all of this weight shifting, I
had loosened the torpedo that was in the tube,

and it slid forward. No problem. Well, except that the new angle of the sub and my hanging onto the torpedo with all my extra gold weight made it *keep* sliding forward.

Now I *had* to let go of the gold . . . either that, or fall to my death. It was another tough decision, but with all the bad publicity death had been getting lately, I decided to let go of the knapsack. I wasn't thrilled as I watched a life's fortune (actually, several life fortunes) drop out of sight into the deep murkiness. But that was nothing compared to my newest and greatest problem. . . . (I hope you're keeping score, 'cause it gets worse.)

The torpedo was *still* moving! My tug and the tilting of the sub were enough to keep the torpedo coming forward, out of the tube.

No problem. All I had to do was get out of the way. Just step aside and watch it fall into the murky depths right behind the knapsack. Simple, right? And it was . . . well, except for one final little problem. . . . (I told you there was more.)

To my surprise, ol' Queeny made an encore appearance. That's right. She had been lurking around the other side of the sub's nose. That's what Eric, Wall Street, and Momma Dolphin had been trying to warn me about!

In a flash, Queeny wrapped one of her long arms around my wrist. (I just hate forward girls, don't you? I mean, I hadn't even asked her to go steady, and she was already holding my hand.) Unfortunately, when she wrapped her arm around my wrist, she also wrapped it around the torpedo.

Uh-oh.

Suddenly, we had become a threesome. The torpedo, me, and Queeny.

Finally, the torpedo slid all the way out of the tube and started falling. And since Queeny and the torpedo and I were like a package deal, we all fell together. Like a rock.

But that was okay. Because finally I could make my move. Finally, I could do what I do best. I tilted back my head and shouted my lungs out:

"AUGHHHHHhhhhhh . . ."

Chapter 9

Greed's Cost

So there I was, falling toward my death at about a zillion miles an hour. My mind raced with all sorts of important information, like: Do fifty-year-old torpedoes blow up when they hit ocean floors? Do twelve-year-old boys? And, most importantly, will God think Queeny and I are dating if we suddenly appear before His throne holding hands?

As I fell toward this certain uncertainty, I heard more grating of steel against rock. I realized the submarine was settling back into its old position. *Great,* I thought, *if you're going to die, it's always best to leave things the way you found them, neat and tidy, so your Mom can be proud at the funeral.*

As we kept falling, the pressure in my ears was going crazy. I wanted to blow against them and clear them, but at the moment I was using

up all my air doing something far more important, like:

"AUGHHHHHHHHHHHHHHHHHH . . ."

Suddenly, out of the corner of my eye, I
caught some movement. Momma and Babe
Dolphin. What were they doing following me?
Didn't they know I was about to turn into a
major explosion—that I was about to change my
identity from "McDoogle the Amazing Moron" to
"McDoogle the Human Mushroom Cloud?"

Momma darted past me once, twice. The
third time, she dropped her nose slightly and
dove directly into ol' Queeny. I'm sure that had
to give my monster girlfriend the world's worst
headache, or stomachache, or somethingache
(it's hard to tell the body parts of monsters).

But Queeny didn't get the message. She still
kept her tentacle wrapped around my arm and
the torpedo. (Breaking up can be so hard to do.)

Momma swam past and dove in again. This
time she made her point—hard, very hard, right
in the center of my death date.

Queeny's arm slithered away, and she
dropped out of sight. Before I could say, "Sorry
we're not going steady anymore, but can we still
be friends?" the torpedo hit one of the rocky
ledges that stuck out.

CLANG!

I closed my eyes, waiting for the explosion. I wanted to miss the gory details, like my body blowing up and being scattered through the entire Pacific Ocean. But nothing happened. No *K-BOOM,* no *K-BANG,* not even a *POP-SIZZLE-SIZZLE.* Nothing.

Still, the fun and games weren't exactly over.

When Queeny let go, I expected to stop falling. But I was moving so fast, and the gold in my swim trunks was so heavy, that I kept right on dropping until I also hit the rocky ledge.

CRASH . . . CRACKLE, BREAK!

The *CRASH* was me landing on the ledge, just a few feet to the right of the torpedo. Unfortunately, I hit a weaker section of the rock which explains the *CRACKLE, BREAK!* That was me breaking through the ledge which, of course, led to more falling fun.

"*AUGHhhhh . . .*"

Finally, there was the familiar and ever faithful: "*OOMPH!*"

I'd hit another, much wider, ledge. Great. That meant there would be no more *CRASH*ings, no more *CRACKLE, BREAK*ings, and definitely no more "*AUGHhhh*"ings. Unfortunately, for the moment, it looked like there would be no more breathing, either. I'd gotten the air completely knocked out of me. Still, some habits are hard to break. After a moment I caught my breath and started inhaling again.

I was pretty dazed as I lay on my back, looking up at the rocks I'd just broken through. They were about eight or ten feet above me. There was plenty of mud and silt and stuff falling, but there was no missing my ol' traveling companion, Mr. Torpedo. He sat on the ledge, teetering directly over my head.

It's true, I had finally finished my little falling routine. But it looked like the torpedo hadn't quite finished its routine. Or maybe it was just lonely and wanted to join me for some company. In any case, as the mud and rocks continued to slide and break away, I knew the torpedo would also be dropping by . . . directly onto me.

Getting tired of the view, I tried to get up, but a sharp pain shot through my legs. Something inside of me was broken. Probably lots of somethings. I tried to crawl, but the ol' legs just didn't feel like cooperating.

I looked back up. The rocks and mud continued to fall—the torpedo continued to teeter.

Great, I thought, *I travel all this way. I do all these things, and for what? To have my entire life reduced to this? A torpedo test target?*

I knew whatever broken bones I had were keeping me from crawling out of the way. But I also knew that if I took the weight of the gold bars out of my swim trunks I could float up and dog-paddle out of there. Of course, that meant leaving behind whatever fortune I had left.

To die or not to die, that is the question.

Reluctantly, I reached for the bars, then stopped. What was I doing? A whole life's fortune and I was just going to throw it away?

More rocks fell.

On second thought, a whole life's fortune without the life can be such an inconvenience.

I looked back up at the torpedo. There were only seconds before it would drop down and make its permanent impression upon me.

I reached into my trunks and pulled out the first bar of gold. It was beautiful and shiny and gorgeous. But it was also deadly. If I hung onto it, I would be one of the richest kids in the world— also one of the deadest. With a deep breath and a heavy sigh, I dropped it. It made a soft crunching sound as it hit the sand beside me.

Suddenly, I was much lighter. *Good,* I thought, *maybe I can at least keep one—*

More rocks fell. I looked up—the torpedo was slipping faster.

I quickly reached in and pulled out the other bar, dropping it to the ground. Bye-bye, riches. Hello, living.

Immediately, I lifted off the ledge and started floating. Good. I could make it, I could get out of the way before the torpedo fell and—

Then I saw it . . . the knapsack I had dropped. It had been lying right behind me. I don't know what came over me (though I suspect it started with the letters *GR*, ended in the letter *D* and had a couple *E*s thrown in somewhere in the middle). In any case, I knew I had to go for the knapsack. I had to try.

I started paddling toward it. I was a lot lighter now, and I had to fight against floating upward. But I slowly made progress. Three feet above, two feet, one—

I was floating directly over it. Unfortunately, it was about this time that the torpedo made its final slip and started falling.

I looked up. I was dead. Gone. McDoogle McNuggets all over the ledge. There was no way I could get out of there in time. I could only stare as everything turned to slow motion—as the torpedo plunged straight toward me—two tons of cold, very hard, "this-is-sure-going-to-smart" steel.

I don't know what happened next. Everything turned kind of blurry and mixed up. I do remember swimming like crazy to get out of there. I also remember looking up and seeing the torpedo so close that I could read the letters on its nose. But what I remember most was Momma Dolphin suddenly darting in. She squeezed herself between the torpedo's nose and me. Then, using the torpedo as leverage, she flipped her tail backward. Hard. So hard that she sent me flying out of the way.

I tumbled and turned. Everything was topsy-turvy confusion. No ups, no downs, just swirling water and bubbles. It seemed to last forever.

Then, when forever was finally over, I realized I had made it. I had survived. I looked down at the ledge. I floated about five feet above it now. Everything was all clouded with mud and silt where the torpedo hit. I glanced up and saw Babe circling above me, around and around. But there was no Momma. I looked every direction, but I still couldn't see her.

I glanced back at Babe. He swam faster and faster, in tight little circles. I didn't get it. What happened? Where was Momma? What was wrong with Babe?

The mud and silt were clearing and I finally made out the torpedo lying on its side. But there was another shape floating beside it. I couldn't believe it. My heart began to pound in my ears. I swam in to get a closer look. If my legs hurt, I didn't feel them. I didn't feel anything . . . except a weight growing deep inside my chest—a weight that got heavier with every foot I approached.

Finally, I was floating directly beside the form.

It was Momma. She had *not* gotten out of the way. The torpedo had slammed her into the ground. Now her body drifted lifelessly in the current. The back of my throat tightened with emotion. Tears burned my eyes as I reached out to touch her. She felt just as slick and rubbery as before. But this time she did not respond to my touch. This time I felt no life.

My chest began to heave. Short spurts of bubbles escaped from my mouth. I was sobbing. To think she had done this for me. She had given up her life to save mine. And for what? For that stupid knapsack, those stupid bars of gold?

Babe approached from the other side. He seemed puzzled, confused. He cautiously nudged his mother with his nose. There was no reaction. He tried again, a little harder, like when they were playing. She still did not move.

Babe pulled back a moment and clicked softly. There was no answer. He tried again, this time stroking her back with his nose.

Nothing.

He continued, his pathetic little squeals and squeaks growing louder. But still no answer.

I tried to touch him, to explain what had happened, but he instinctively pulled away. It was almost like he knew I was the one to blame. I turned back to his mother's body. My tears were coming faster now.

I don't know how long we stayed like that, Babe and I, looking down at Momma. But finally something took hold of my shoulder. At first I figured it was Queeny. *That's okay,* I thought, *I deserve to die.* But it wasn't Queeny. It was a couple of the divers from *The Bulwinkle.* I guess Eric had radioed that I was in trouble, and they had come down to get me. One of them was pointing at his wristwatch and my regulator, motioning that I was running out of air.

He was right, of course. But at the moment I didn't much care. He grabbed my shoulder even tighter. I tried to resist, pointing to Momma, trying to explain that I needed to stay to help.

They both shook their heads, making it clear there was nothing more I could do. Whatever was done, was done. I reached out to touch Momma one last time. I tenderly patted her on the head. *I'm sorry, old girl, I'm so sorry.*

Then, ever so gently, they pulled me away, and we began our swim toward the surface.

Chapter 10

Wrapping Up

The best Captain Ray could make of my legs was that one was broken and the other pretty bruised. But we wouldn't know for sure until we entered port and saw a doctor. In the meantime, the guys had rigged up a splint for my one leg and loaned me a makeshift crutch to get around.

The sun was just starting to set. All of the commotion had died down. The minisub had been loaded, and we were about to get underway. I was leaning against the rail when Eric passed by and asked, "You okay? You look a little pale."

I nodded, leaned over the railing, and did what I did best for that time of day. I heaved my guts out.

Eric glanced away to give me some privacy. "You're sure getting good at that," he said, trying to lighten the mood.

"I've had lots of practice."

He looked at his watch. "But you're a little late this afternoon. Must be all the excitement, or the storm."

I glanced at him and rolled my eyes. Luckily, the storm had skirted around us and had never entirely hit. But that didn't stop the waves from rolling in. For the past hour or so the phrase "rock-'n'-roll" had taken on a whole new meaning. But I wasn't sick because of the waves or the excitement or the time of day. I was sick because of what I had done.

There was a loud banging and clanking of iron hitting steel. I turned to watch one of the crew members cranking up the anchor. *The Bulwinkle's* engine revved, she gave a little shudder, and we were on our way.

"We'll be in port by midnight," Eric offered.

I looked back out at the water and shook my head. "How could I have been so stupid?"

"Hey, we were both stupid. It was my idea, remember?"

I continued shaking my head, barely hearing. "Risking my life; doing all those dumb, dangerous things. And for what? A bunch of gold?"

Eric took a deep breath. "Remember what I said a couple of days back when *The Sea Witch* first threatened us? Remember how I said greed makes people do weird things?"

I nodded.

"Lawyers, hard hats, farmers, even sailors—put a little money in front of us and watch out, we go crazy."

I nodded again and gave a hearty sniff. "My pastor is always quoting from the Bible. He says, 'The love of money is the root of all evil.'"

Eric took a deep breath and looked out over the ocean. "He may be right," he sighed. "He just may be right."

Suddenly, I saw the splash of water off the stern. My heart leaped. "Look," I shouted. "It's her. It's the mother dolphin!"

Eric turned and took a hard look. Then he sadly shook his head. "That's not the mom, Wally, that's the kid. See how small he is? And check out the markings."

Of course, Eric was right; it was Babe. And, of course, I felt even worse. Now the little guy was totally alone, orphaned. And he had one person and one person only to thank for it—me. I looked down at the railing, feeling my eyes start to burn again.

"Hold it. Wait a minute," Eric said, still looking.

I glanced back up.

"That's not just one dolphin," Eric's voice grew excited. "There's two. There are two dolphins out there!"

I peered hard, straining for all I was worth to see. He was right! There *were* two dolphins! The first one, Babe, was doing all of the jumping and splashing—but there was definitely a second one. It was staying more under the water and doing a lot less jumping, but it was definitely there.

"Is it . . ." I swallowed back the excitement, trying not to hope too hard. "Is it her?"

Eric brought his binoculars up to his face and looked. My eyes shot from him to the dolphins, and back to him again. Finally, he broke into a smile and began to nod.

"It's her!"

He handed the binoculars to me. "See for yourself."

I grabbed them and looked. Sure enough, there was Babe leaping all around, and beside him was . . . Momma. She was a lot less energetic than before, but she was definitely moving.

My heart swelled. I gripped the binoculars tighter and continued to stare. "I thought she was dead," I said. "I mean, her eyes were closed, and she definitely wasn't breathing—"

"Dolphins are mammals, Wally, they don't breathe under water."

"But she wasn't moving."

"I guess she was just stunned, maybe knocked unconscious."

I continued to stare as Babe did his jumps and circles all around his momma like he was really happy. I guess he had a reason to be. "Do you think she's okay?" I asked. "I mean, she's not doing any jumping or anything."

Eric chuckled. "I imagine she's got herself quite a headache. I probably wouldn't be jumping around if I got hit on the head with a torpedo, either."

"Eric!" It was Captain Ray calling from the pilot house. The man was not happy. In fact, he had that same glare Dad has when he discovers Mom's been using his razor on her legs. "Eric, get up here. We've got a few things to discuss!"

"Here it comes," Eric muttered under his breath. "Wish me luck."

I looked up at him from the binoculars. "Good luck."

He turned and headed up the deck. Neither of us knew what the Captain would say or do to him. But since Eric had already confessed that it was his idea for me to go into the water, chances are he wasn't going to be receiving any medals. I knew my punishment would probably be just as bad. Though I hoped to get time off for being a kid and, of course, for being a world-class Dorkoid.

Suddenly, I smelled deep-fried, grease-saturated chips. It was coming from behind me. "Hey, Opera," I called without turning around.

"How'd you know *(MUNCH, MUNCH, MUNCH)* it was me?" he asked.

"Lucky guess." I turned to see both Opera and Wall Street approaching.

"Did you hear the news?" Wall Street grumbled.

I shook my head.

Opera explained. "The Mexican government *(MUNCH, MUNCH, MUNCH)* was monitoring our communications with *The Sea Witch*. They just called Uncle Ray. They'll be coming out to pick up the gold."

"They can't do that," I protested.

"Sure they can," Opera said munching away. "The money came from their country."

"But I'm the one who found it!"

"That's why they promised to send you a thank-you letter."

It was weird, but even now, after all I'd been through, I was still trying to hang on to the gold. "But, but, but—"

Before I continued my motorboat imitation, Wall Street interrupted. "Relax, Wally. We'll hire some hot-shot attorney and take it to court.

I mean, if they want to play hardball, we can play hardball." Her voice was getting louder and shriller, the way it always did when she got excited or talked about money (which was almost always). "You'll get the best lawyer money can buy. You'll sue them; you'll make them wish they'd never even heard of—"

"Wall Street," I said, raising my hand. I had just turned back to watch Momma and Babe off in the distance. Things had suddenly come back into focus.

She continued, "First you'll hit them with a lawsuit."

"Wall Street."

"Then you'll pull in the North American Free Trade folks."

"Wall Street."

"Then you'll—"

"WALL STREET!"

She looked up at me, startled.

"Forget it," I said.

"I'm sorry," she said, shaking out her ear with her finger. "It almost sounded like you said, 'Forget it.'"

"I did. The gold, the money . . . let it go. I'm not doing anything."

For once in her life, Wall Street had no comeback. She could only stare at me as if I had just punched her in the gut. In a sense, maybe I had. But I'd been through too much. I'd seen too many things. Most of all, I had learned an important truth: Greed is evil. There are no two ways about it. It sneaks up without you even noticing. And if you let it hang around, if you keep feeding it, it will take control and ruin everything.

Wall Street's mouth hung open as if she were in shock. Maybe she was. Opera took a deep breath and sighed between munchings. "Too bad. All that hard work . . . and for what?" He took another deep breath. "Nothing."

I looked back out over the stern. By now Momma and Babe were just little specks. In one sense I knew Opera was right. But in another, I knew he was wrong. Because I had gained something. I had learned that, by itself, there's nothing wrong with money. But if you get to loving it too much, it can be deadly.

I adjusted my crutch and started to hobble off. "I'm going below to finish the story I'm writing. You guys coming?"

Opera nodded and followed. But Wall Street stayed glued to the railing, looking down into the water, still a little numb.

"Wall Street," I said. "Wall Street, are you okay?"

She said nothing, but continued to stare.

"She'll be fine," Opera said. "For her *(MUNCH, MUNCH, MUNCH)*, losing all that money is kind of like losing a loved one. Maybe lots of loved ones. But she'll get over it. In a few months, she'll be as good as new."

I gave him a look.

He shrugged. "And you, too." He popped another chip into his mouth. "In a few months you'll forget this whole thing ever happened."

"I hope not," I said as I turned and headed toward our cabin. "I hope I remember this for the rest of my life."

Back in Proverb Guy's flying fly swatter, it's a fight to the finish. Our hero must destroy this bad guy's evil Excuse-a-tron, or the world will never have another excuse again. Refrigerator repairmen will have to show up on time, car mechanics will have to have the parts, and news reporters will have to tell the whole truth.

As they fight back and forth, they accidentally crash into the control panel, pushing the button that reads:

WARNING: DO NOT PUSH THIS BUTTON

Suddenly, the fly swatter takes a nosedive, heading downward faster than a kid's smile after learning he has to go to summer school.

The two try everything to pull the nose up, but nothing works. Faster and faster they fall toward certain death. And then, just when it looks like you're getting cheated out of a cool ending to this story, the fly swatter's front doorbell rings.

"Who is it?" Proverb Guy cries.

"Telegram!" a voice from the other side shouts.

"Listen, can you come back a little later? We're kind of busy right now."

"It'll only take a second!"

Proverb Guy looks at our hero and shrugs. "Sorry, it might be something important."

Gnat Man nods in superhero understanding and steps back to let Proverb Guy answer the door. When he opens it, he is met by glaring lights, TV cameras, and a smiling Ed McMoan handing him a check.

"Congratulations!" McMoan shouts over the roaring wind. "You've just won a million dollars from our Peering House Sweepstakes."

"I don't believe it!" Proverb Guy yells, trying to look surprised for the cameras. "Why, I've never won anything in my whole life!"

"What are you going to do with all that money?" McMoan shouts.

"Know any life insurance salesmen?" Gnat Man yells.

"What?" Proverb Guy shouts back.

"All that money's okay, but we've got more important things to do."

"Like what?"

"Oh, how 'bout living!" Gnat Man points to the approaching ground. "I don't want to be a spoilsport, but we only have 3.2 seconds of life, make that 2.8, uh 2.3..."

"I see your point." Proverb Guy turns to McMoan and shouts, "Sorry, not interested." He slams the door and spins back to Gnat Man. "Now, where were we?"

"You were standing over here." Gnat Man repositions him next to the control panel. "And I had my hands around your throat like this. And—leapin' ladybugs! What's that?" Gnat Man points to another button labeled:

EMERGENCY STOP
Use Only If You've Accidentally Pushed The "Warning: Do Not Push" Button.

Both of them leap for the button and push it. As luck would have it (along with some mighty clever writing on my part), the flying fly swatter screeches to a halt just inches from the ground.

"Whew," Gnat Man sighs, "that was close."

"I'll say," Proverb Guy agrees. "Not only did we almost die, but my Nolan Ryan baseball card would have been destroyed."

"You've got Nolan Ryan?"

"Right here," Proverb Guy says with a grin as he pulls out the tattered card from his back pocket.

"Wow, that is so cool," Gnat Man says as he opens up the fly swatter's door and steps out onto the ground.

"I've got an Orel Hershiser back at the Gnat Cave."

Proverb Guy climbs out after him. "No kidding, I didn't know you collected baseball cards."

"For years. Say, you don't happen to have a Reggie Jackson, do you?"

"Nah, I don't have one. I have two."

"Two? What could I trade you for one?"

"What do you have?"

"Come on over to the Gnat Cave, and I'll show you."

"Great. Want to grab a bite to eat first?"

"Why not."

"How 'bout some Chinese?"

"Sounds super keen."

And so the once-mortal enemies stroll off together, arm in arm. Well, in Gnat Man's case, many arms in many arms.

"Sorry about your losing all that sweepstakes money," Gnat Man says.

"Don't worry about it. There are some things more important than money."

"Like a Bo Jackson card?"

"You've got Bo Jackson?!"

As they stroll into the sunset, you are no doubt asking what will become of the evil Excuse-a-tron and all the excuses it has stored up. Not to worry. It may take awhile to bring the world's level of excuses back up to normal, but as long as there are kids and unfinished homework, teenagers coming home late from dates, and long-distance telephone companies claiming you'll save money when you change over to them...well, dear reader, there will always be excuses.

You'll want to read them all.

THE INCREDIBLE WORLDS OF WALLY McDOOGLE

#1—My Life As a Smashed Burrito with Extra Hot Sauce

Twelve-year-old Wally—the "Walking Disaster Area"—is forced to stand up to Camp Wahkah Wahkah's number one all-American bad guy. One hilarious mishap follows another until, fighting together for their very lives, Wally learns the need for even his worst enemy to receive Jesus Christ. (ISBN 0-8499-3402-8 softcover; ISBN 1-4003-0571-3 hardcover)

#2—My Life As Alien Monster Bait

"Hollyweird" comes to Middletown! Wally's a superstar! A movie company has chosen our hero to be eaten by their mechanical "Mutant from Mars"! It's a close race as to which will consume Wally first—the disaster-plagued special effects "monster" or his own out-of-control pride—until he learns the cost of true friendship and of God's command for humility. (ISBN 0-8499-3403-6 softcover; ISBN 1-4003-0572-1 hardcover)

#3—My Life As a Broken Bungee Cord

A hot-air balloon race! What could be more fun? Then again, we're talking about Wally McDoogle, the "Human Catastrophe." Calamity builds on calamity until, with his life on the line, Wally learns what it means to FULLY put his trust in God. (ISBN 0-8499-3404-4 softcover; ISBN 1-4003-0573-X hardcover)

#4—My Life As Crocodile Junk Food

Wally visits missionary friends in the South American rain forest. Here he stumbles onto a whole new set of impossible predicaments . . . until he understands the need and joy of sharing Jesus Christ with others. (ISBN 0-8499-3405-2 softcover; ISBN 1-4003-0613-2 hardcover)

#5—My Life As Dinosaur Dental Floss

A practical joke snowballs into near disaster. After prehistoric-size mishaps and a talk with the President, Wally learns that honesty really is the best policy. (ISBN 0-8499-3537-7 softcover; ISBN 1-4003-0614-0 hardcover)

#6—My Life As a Torpedo Test Target
Wally uncovers the mysterious secrets of a sunken submarine. As dreams of fame and glory increase, so do the famous McDoogle mishaps. Besides hostile sea creatures, hostile pirates, and hostile Wally McDoogle clumsiness, there is the war against his own greed and selfishness. It isn't until Wally finds himself on a wild ride atop a misguided torpedo that he realizes the source of true greatness. (ISBN 0-8499-3538-5 softcover; ISBN 1-4003-0638-8 hardcover)

#7—My Life As a Human Hockey Puck
Look out . . . Wally McDoogle turns athlete! Jealousy and envy drive Wally from one hilarious calamity to another until, as the team's mascot, he learns humility while suddenly being thrown in to play goalie for the Middletown Super Chickens! (ISBN 0-8499-3601-2 softcover; ISBN 1-4003-0639-6 hardcover)

#8—My Life As an Afterthought Astronaut
"Just 'cause I didn't follow the rules doesn't make it my fault that the Space Shuttle almost crashed. Well, okay, maybe it was sort of my fault. But not the part when Pilot O'Brien was spacewalking and I accidentally knocked him halfway to Jupiter. . . ." So begins another hilarious Wally McDoogle MISadventure as our boy blunder stows aboard the Space Shuttle and learns the importance of: Obeying the Rules! (ISBN 0-8499-3602-0 softcover; ISBN 1-4003-0729-5 hardcover)

#9—My Life As Reindeer Road Kill
Santa on an out-of-control four wheeler? Electrical Rudolph on the rampage? Nothing unusual, just Wally McDoogle doing some last-minute Christmas shopping . . . FOR GOD! Our boy blunder dreams that an angel has invited him to a birthday party for Jesus. Chaos and comedy follow as he turns the town upside down looking for the perfect gift, until he finally bumbles his way into the real reason for the season. (ISBN 0-8499-3866-X softcover; ISBN 1-4003-0730-9 hardcover)

#10—My Life As a Toasted Time Traveler
Wally travels back from the future to warn himself of an upcoming accident. But before he knows it, there are more Wallys running around than even Wally himself can handle. Catastrophes reach an all-time high as Wally tries to out-think God and rewrite history. (ISBN 0-8499-3867-8 softcover; ISBN 1-4003-0731-7 hardcover)

#11—My Life As Polluted Pond Scum

This laugh-filled Wally disaster includes: a monster lurking in the depths of a mysterious lake . . . a glowing figure with powers to summon the creature to the shore . . . and one Wally McDoogle, who reluctantly stumbles upon the truth. Wally's entire town is in danger. He must race against the clock and his own fears and learn to trust God before he has any chance of saving the day. (ISBN 0-8499-3875-9)

#12—My Life As a Bigfoot Breath Mint

Wally gets his big break to star with his uncle Max in the famous Fantasmo World stunt show. Unlike his father, whom Wally secretly suspects to be a major loser, Uncle Max is everything Wally longs to be . . . or so it appears. But Wally soon discovers the truth and learns who the real hero is in his life. (ISBN 0-8499-3876-7)

#13—My Life As a Blundering Ballerina

Wally agrees to switch places with Wall Street. Everyone is in on the act as the two try to survive seventy-two hours in each other's shoes and learn the importance of respecting other people. (ISBN 0-8499-4022-2)

#14—My Life As a Screaming Skydiver

Master of mayhem Wally turns a game of laser tag into international espionage. From the Swiss Alps to the African plains, Agent 00½th bumblingly employs such top-secret gizmos as rocket-powered toilet paper, exploding dental floss, and the ever-popular transformer tacos to stop the dreaded and super secret . . . Giggle Gun. (ISBN 0-8499-4023-0)

#15—My Life As a Human Hairball

When Wally and Wall Street visit a local laboratory, they are accidentally miniaturized and swallowed by some unknown stranger. It is a race against the clock as they fly through various parts of the body in a desperate search for a way out while learning how wonderfully we're made. (ISBN 0-8499-4024-9)

#16—My Life As a Walrus Whoopee Cushion

Wally and his buddies, Opera and Wall Street, win the Gazillion Dollar Lotto! Everything is great, until they realize they lost the ticket at the zoo! Add some bungling bad guys, a zoo break-in, the release of all the animals, a SWAT team or two . . . and you have the usual McDoogle mayhem as Wally learns the dangers of greed. (ISBN 0-8499-4025-7)

#17—My Life As a Computer Cockroach
(formerly *My Life As a Mixed-Up Millennium Bug*)
When Wally accidentally fries the circuits of Ol' Betsy, his beloved laptop computer, suddenly whatever he types turns into reality! At 11:59, New Year's Eve, Wally tries retyping the truth into his computer—which shorts out every other computer in the world. By midnight, the entire universe has credited Wally's mishap to the MILLENNIUM BUG! Panic, chaos, and hilarity start the new century, thanks to our beloved boy blunder. (ISBN 0-8499-4026-5)

#18—My Life As a Beat-Up Basketball Backboard
Ricko Slicko's Advertising Agency claims that they can turn the dorkiest human in the world into the most popular. And who better to prove this than our boy blunder, Wally McDoogle! Soon he has his own TV series and fans wearing glasses just like his. But when he tries to be a star athlete for his school basketball team, Wally finally learns that being popular isn't all it's cut out to be. (ISBN 0-8499-4027-3)

#19—My Life As a Cowboy Cowpie
Once again our part-time hero and full-time walking disaster area finds himself smack-dab in another misadventure. This time it's full of dude-ranch disasters, bungling broncobusters, and the world's biggest cow—well, let's just say it's not a pretty picture (or a pleasant-smelling one). Through it all, Wally learns the dangers of seeking revenge. (ISBN 0-8499-5990-X)

#20—My Life As Invisible Intestines
When Wally becomes invisible, he can do whatever he wants, like humiliating bullies, or helping the local football team win. But the fun is short-lived when everyone from a crazy ghostbuster to the *59 1/2 Minutes* TV show to the neighbor's new dog begin pursuing him. Soon Wally is stumbling through another incredible disaster . . . until he finally learns that cheating and taking shortcuts in life are not all they're cracked up to be and that honesty really is the best policy. (ISBN 0-8499-5991-8)

#21—My Life As a Skysurfing Skateboarder
Our boy blunder finds himself participating in the Skateboard Championship of the Universe. (It would be "of the World," except for the one kid who claims to be from Jupiter—a likely story, in spite of his two heads and seven arms.) Amid the incredible chaotic chaos by incurably corrupt competitors (say that five times fast), Wally learns there is more to life than winning. (ISBN 0-8499-5592-6)

#22—My Life As a Tarantula Toe Tickler

Trying to be more independent, Wally hides a minor mistake. But minor mistakes lead to major mishaps! Soon Wally begins working for Junior Genius (the boy super-inventor from book #21), and becomes a human guinea pig to backfiring experiments such as Tina, the giggling tarantula whom he accidentally grows to the size of a small house. Now, our boy blunder must save Tina, his life, and the entire city. Through all of this, Wally learns the importance of admitting mistakes, taking responsibility for his own actions, and always telling the truth. (ISBN 0-8499-5993-4)

#23—My Life As a Prickly Porcupine from Pluto

It's just a little cheating on a little test. There's nothing wrong with that, right? WRONG! So begins another McDoogle disaster as one lie leads to a bigger lie and a bigger lie and even a bigger lie. Soon the entire world believes Wally is an outer-space alien (who looks like a giant porcupine) trying to take over the planet. He is pursued by tanks, helicopters, even a guided missile or two—not to mention his old friends at S.O.S. (Save Our Snails) who, unfortunately, are now trying to save him! It is another hair-raising (er, make that quill-raising) misadventure as our boy blunder learns that honesty really is the best policy. (ISBN 0-8499-5994-2)

#24—My Life As a Splatted-Flat Quarterback

What if every time you made fun of somebody you suddenly acted like them, looked like them, and were treated like them? This time our bungling hero, Wally McDoogle, runs into trouble by unfairly judging others. One mistaken identity builds to another until Wally finds himself playing star quarterback in the Super Bowl. It's not until he tries seeing people through the eyes of God that he realizes it's better to love than to judge. (ISBN 0-8499-5995-0)

#25—My Life As a Belching Baboon with Bad Breath

Wally's got a bad case of the "I wants!" All his friends have way cooler stuff than he has, and he hates it. Even his prayers have turned into, "Dear God, gimme, gimme, gimme, oh yeah, and gimme some more." Until Dad drags him and the family along on an aid project to Africa . . . until he gets lost in the wilderness . . . until he's attacked by hiccupping hippos, rampaging rhinos, and a herd of baboons who definitely don't brush after every meal . . . until he meets a boy his age who shows him what really counts in life and the key to real happiness. (ISBN 1-4003-0634-5)

Guys (and Guyettes)!

Want to hear from me,
the Human Walking Disaster Area,
each week about more misadventures
and the stuff I'm learning in the Bible?

There'll also be riddles to solve
and chances to win prizes!

Log onto www.BillMyers.com and click
on the Wally McDoogle Fan Club icon for
more information and how to join!

Hope to hear from ya!

Wally